I0538304

Homicide and a Happy New Year

Cherryville Cozy Mysteries, Volume 2

Ellie McDougan

Published by Cherryville Titles, 2022.

HOMICIDE AND A HAPPY NEW YEAR

First edition. December 22, 2022.

Copyright © 2022 Ellie McDougan.

ISBN: 978-0645667431

Written by Ellie McDougan.

Table of Contents

Chapter 1...1

Chapter 2...9

Chapter 3..15

Chapter 4..21

Chapter 5..29

Chapter 6..35

Chapter 7..41

Chapter 8..47

Chapter 9..53

Chapter 10..59

Chapter 11..65

Chapter 12..71

Chapter 13..77

Chapter 14..83

Chapter 15..89

Chapter 16..95

Chapter 17.. 101

Chapter 18.. 107

Chapter 19.. 113

Chapter 20.. 119

Chapter 21.. 125

Chapter 22.. 129

Chapter 23 | Victims and Valentine's Day - Coming soon!........ 135

Thank you to my parents, for your loving support, always. And for letting me knock about your house at 4:30 am when I come to visit, working on my funny writing projects. I try not to be too much of a clutz in the dark.

Also, thank you to my writing friends: Beth, Paola, Teal, Alix and Clare for tuning in to my adventures from across the world.

Thank you also to the magical Plot Genie, Heather Cardona. A big thank you again to my book cover designer, Donna Rogers and my beta reader and Copyeditors, Nichole Heydenburg and Dr. Elizabeth Houlihan.

Chapter 1

"Goodness, I think I've eaten too much again," said Grace Beaumont, yawning, as she put her feet up on a comfortable footrest. "I can't believe that I ate the last of the Christmas cookies." She smoothed her hand over her stomach.

It was Boxing Day, the day after Christmas, and Belle was enjoying having some time off. After working nonstop at the hot chocolate booth for the last six weeks, it was nice to relax and take a break.

"They were good cookies," agreed Belle, curling her legs up under her, as she snuggled under a knitted blanket on the couch.

"I'm glad everyone had a good time on Christmas Day," said her grandmother from her recliner as she sipped her snowberry tea. "It's lovely having visitors, but it's even better when you can sit by your own fire and relax. Now that it's just the two of us, we can celebrate however we want." She tucked the little crocheted blanket around her legs with a happy sigh.

Mittens meowed in agreement as he took the opportunity of jumping onto Grace's lap and making himself comfortable. His little feet kneaded industriously.

Belle took a sip of her own tea. She snuggled deeper under her own blanket and watched the pine cones in the fire crackle and pop.

"I'm going to have to start working out more."

Belle chuckled. "Now, Gram, you know that you don't need to work out more. You're as thin as ever."

Grace huffed. "You're just saying that because you know that I'll take you up on your offer to be my personal trainer."

Belle laughed again. "I think you're perfect just the way you are."

Grace reached over to pat her granddaughter's hand. "I think you're perfect just the way you are, too."

Belle watched her grandmother yawn and close her eyes for a moment. "Thanks, Gram," she replied, her forehead creasing with

1

concern. She had noticed that Grace was increasingly tired these days. It was to be expected. Over the past year, her slow-growing cancer had required regular treatments at the local clinic. Thankfully, things were in remission. For now. Grace could go for longer periods without a visit to her doctor. However, Belle still lived in a constant state of alert, in case the dreaded condition returned.

And then there were the medical bills.

The costs of Gram's hospital visits had been more than expected. Belle's brain was constantly working on how to make sure that they had enough money to pay the debt. It felt like trying to solve an elusive clue for a crossword puzzle, but never quite getting the answer.

The scent of pine permeated the house, and not just from the burning pine cones in the fireplace. Their Christmas tree was still in the corner of the living room, its green boughs laden with various ornaments, shimmering tinsel, and sparkling lights. Soon, they would be taking down the decorations and packing them away, but not yet.

Belle's eyes fell upon the star at the top of the tree, its wooden surface painted with gold paint, now a little scratched and worn. She had made it herself with the help of her Gram several years ago. It was a tradition in Belle's family to put up a Christmas tree early and to spend time together every year making more decorations to add to their collection. Even though her parents had passed away when Belle was quite young, they had carried on the tradition every year. This year, they had made little dangly icicles and snowflakes from beads and sequins. The sequins caught the light from the fire and reflected it in dancing patterns on the wall.

Mittens also loved the new glittery decorations, possibly a little too much. He particularly enjoyed knocking the them off the tree and batting them about on the floorboards.

Outside, snowflakes were gently falling, blanketing the town in a soft white eiderdown of cold fluff. Belle could see the twinkly lights strung out on the porch banister winking on and off.

Grace had picked up her knitting and her needles clicked together as she worked on a new project, a scarf for Belle. Belle watched as her grandmother worked the needles, admiring her nimble fingers.

"So, what are you going to do now, Belle?" Grace stroked Mittens, who had woken up and started purring loudly. "Your year was so busy with different jobs, but it's over now. What are you going to do next?"

It was true. Belle's work at the hot chocolate booth at Harvey's Christmas Tree Farm was finished. Instead of harvesting trees for sale, Harvey was now getting ready to plant them in the spring.

Belle gazed into the fire. "I don't really know," she admitted. She had been thinking about it for some time now, but every time she tried to come up with an idea, nothing seemed right.

Harvey had generously offered Belle short-term work sorting out his messy office, but that work may only be available in February. Plus, as soon as his office was tidy, there would be no more need for Belle's administrative services and she would be back to square one, looking for employment.

She tried not to worry about it too much. But if Belle was honest, the thought of what she would do next had been worrying her a lot. Not that she wanted her grandmother to know that. The last thing she wanted Grace to do was worry about money.

"I'm going to look for a new job in a couple of days," said Belle decisively. She set her cup of tea on the table beside the couch. "There will be lots of places hiring when the new year starts. We'll just have to watch our pennies until then."

"You're right," said Grace, finishing her row of stitches, turning her knitting and starting on another. "I was thinking that I could ask the women at the Guild whether they know of anyone needing to hire staff."

"The Cherryville Women's Guild?" Belle wrinkled her nose. "I think that it's better not to get them involved."

The Women's Guild was an organization of women who met once a week to knit, crochet, and gossip like old hens. Grace went there every week for the companionship and the conversation.... Conversation that usually involved small-town news and gossip.

For instance, the Women's Guild had once gotten wind that a new girl in town was looking for a boyfriend. They had immediately tried to match her up with all of their sons and nephews. The poor girl had been set up on such a string of blind dates that she had desperately signed up for online dating just to get away from their good intentions. In no time, she had found a boyfriend for herself. One who lived in another town.

"But they might know of someone who is hiring," persisted Grace. "It can't hurt to ask."

"It sure could," said Belle. "You know Wilma and her organizational abilities. She'll call a town meeting to discuss my job opportunities. Before we know it, everyone in Cherryville will know about our business. I don't want people knowing what's going on with us."

Wilma Figg was the President of the Women's Guild and she liked to organize the lives of everyone in town, usually to their detriment. Wilma's enthusiasm for helping people, whether they wanted the help or not, usually ended in a complete mess.

Grace nodded. She had only been half serious about involving the Women's Guild in finding Belle a new job. "Okay. I won't ask Wilma to find you a job. You know, I really wish that I could help bring in money for my medical bills. I wish I could go back to teaching, but I just don't have the energy anymore."

Grace had previously worked as a teacher at the local high school, and the children had adored her. She had retired a few years ago when her health had started to decline.

"There are plenty of other things that you could do," said Belle, trying to cheer her up. "You're always so good at crafts. Why don't you sell them online?"

"Oh, I don't know," said Grace, stroking Mittens' soft fur as he lay purring in the crook of her arm. "I really enjoy doing my crafts in my own time, rather than working to a deadline. I don't think my arthritic fingers could keep up with that much knitting."

She picked up her a flyer and handed it to Belle. "I could always apply for this job at the winery," she joked. "Or you could. You're good at making friends."

"The winery?" asked Belle, frowning at the flyer in the dim light from the fire. "Would that be the Buchen Winery? That fancy place just out of town?" She turned over the page.

The flyer was indeed for the Buchen Winery. They were hosting a New Year's celebration, and they were looking for staff for the party and then to work for the whole of January, serving wine to tourists. She had heard about the place, but to be honest, it was too fancy for many of the blue-collar people of Cherryville to visit. It was a bit of a drive out of town and Mr. Buchen hired most of their staff from out of state anyway. In fact, the Buchen Winery was a bit of an enigma. Belle didn't know anyone from Cherryville who had worked there.

"Well, as long as there are no dead bodies for me to find in unexpected places, that sounds perfect!" joked Belle, passing the flyer back.

After discovering the dead body of a woman in a dumpster at her last job, and helping the sheriff to catch the killer, Belle was happy to find a job that was boring and normal. "There have been no murders at the Buchen Winery, have there?"

"No. Not that I know of. But it mentions something about understanding wines," said her grandmother, squinting at the small print. "What does that mean? How much is there to understand? You open the bottle and you drink it."

Belle shrugged. "I guess there are different wines to learn about. It says they're willing to train the right person."

"Well," said her Gram, frowning. "It would be a change from working outside in the cold. Better than running a hot chocolate booth in the snow."

Belle smiled. "It would." The warmth from the fireplace was soothing, and she could feel her eyelids getting heavy. She yawned and stretched.

"You could phone them tomorrow morning," said Grace, as the hall clock chimed ten times. She nodded at Belle's nearly empty mug of tea. "I think it's time for bed."

Belle got up from the couch, folded the knitted blanket, and gave Mittens a pat. "Okay, I'm going upstairs. I'll see you in the morning."

"Okay, goodnight," said her Gram, smiling as she got to her feet to give Belle a hug. "I hope that you sleep well."

Even though she was sleepy, she felt a small thrill of excitement about the prospect of working at a winery. It would be a fun change and she would get to learn more about something new: wines. Even better, it would be a *normal* job that didn't involve standing in the snow or solving murders.

Belle read the job advert again and circled the number for the winery with a pen. She would call them first thing tomorrow morning. The advert said a short phone interview was all that was needed.

As Belle got ready for bed, she pondered what she would need in order to serve wines. She would need a uniform, for sure. No doubt she would be required to wear all black, like most places. She thought about the bills that were due in January and wondered how much the Buchen Winery paid their short-term staff.

Just as she was about to switch off the light, Mittens jumped onto the end of her bed.

"How much do you know about wines?" she asked him in the darkness.

Mittens purred in response.

"Me neither," she said. "But then again, how hard could it be?"

Chapter 2

Four days later and Belle was standing in the staffroom of the Buchen Winery, along with about fifteen strangers.

"... and I want everyone to have learned about our wines and to demonstrate that knowledge to each of our guests when required," Mr. Buchen was saying to all of the serving staff gathered around him. His light gray trousers were neatly pressed and the scent of strong cologne wafted around from him. To Belle, he looked and sounded like a wealthy, balding man from a European country somewhere.

It had taken Belle about an hour to drive out to the place, being located past some of the cherry farms in the area, in a picturesque part of the country. As a wine-making business, the Buchen Winery had been in operation since the early nineteenth century. For the past ten years, it had hosted an exclusive annual New Year's Eve party. Attendance was by invitation only, and only the wealthy and well-connected were invited.

"We've got a variety of wines, starting with our basic young vintages and moving up to more our complex older wines." He continued his introductory lecture to the staff. "There will be over twenty different vintages available, and several of them are from our farm. You must read through the printouts given to you and be knowledgeable about the wines. You can test samples of each of the vintages in the tasting room."

Belle's heart sank. Within minutes of arriving at the winery, she had realized how much she didn't know about wines. All she knew was that red wines were good with meat and white wines were better with fish. At least that was what her grandmother had told her.

She looked around at her co-workers. They all seemed to know exactly what they were doing.

Her wandering attention was drawn back to her new boss. "... and that brings me to the end of this introduction." Mr. Buchen closed his notebook.

Belle panicked a little when she realized that she had just missed what the man had said about the samples.

"The most important thing," Mr. Buchen emphasized, "is that you focus on giving our guests the best experience possible. Many of them will have traveled a long way to get here. The more time that we can get them to spend here at the winery, tasting all of our vintages and enjoying our gourmet food options, the more likely they will be to return. Repeat business. That is what we want. And it all depends on... All of you." He pointed at each of them sternly, punctuating his words with finger jabs. "Knowing. Your. Stuff."

Belle blanched.

I don't know any stuff!

There were a few bored nods from the other servers, who looked like they had heard it all before.

Belle swallowed as Mr. Buchen handed out sheafs of papers to everyone in the room.

Why did I ever think that I could handle this job?

"Now, we will be going to the tasting room, I'll show you where everything is and we can go through what I expect from my staff. Everyone, please ensure that you read up on this year's wines tonight. We need everything to go without a hitch at the party tomorrow night."

Belle glanced nervously at the server standing next to her, a pretty girl with auburn hair in a high ponytail. She didn't look fazed by the stack of papers in her hands and Belle guessed that she must already have plenty of experience in the wine industry.

The young woman turned and looked Belle up and down. "You're scared," she said. "Don't freak out. He always makes us do this before the New Year's Party. Just learn it all off by heart. It's not that bad."

"Thanks," Belle whispered back. "I've never worked at a winery before."

"He pays well at least." The auburn-haired server sniffed.

"But before we break off for the educational tasting," Mr. Buchen said. "I would like to introduce you all to our newest member of staff." He waved vaguely in Belle's direction. "Please, everyone introduce yourself to Belle. She will be our newest sommelier for the next few weeks. Please show her the ropes." Then he nodded and led the way out of the room, clipboard in hand.

Everyone slowly turned to look at Belle, and she stared back, nervously. "Hello," she said awkwardly, trying to sound confident. "I'm from Cherryville."

Her fellow servers all looked like a bunch of bored twenty-somethings on college break, who had signed up for some kind of work experience project. They didn't look like people who needed a job. A few of them said "hi" disinterestedly and then followed Mr. Buchen.

"What's a sommelier?" Belle whispered to the auburn-haired server.

She frowned. "You don't know?"

Belle shook her head dumbly. "I don't really drink much wine."

"Geez, he reduced to hiring anyone these days." The girl took a deep breath. "A sommelier is a wine expert," she explained, a patronizing tone creeping into her voice.

"A wine expert?" repeated Belle, surprised. "I thought we were just pouring wine for people at tables."

"No. A sommelier is much more than that. A sommelier looks after all the wines for a restaurant and knows everything about them. It's a prestigious role. But I guess you don't know that either. Didn't the boss tell you this in your interview?"

Belle shook her head. "Afraid not. Mr. Buchen didn't ask me many questions on the phone the other day. He just wanted to know if I could start immediately. He said everyone else was busy. And he hung up pretty quickly."

"Well, consider this a crash course in wine." The girl looked down at her. "Good luck." She laughed softly.

Belle's face must have shown that she didn't think it was all that funny.

"Oh well," the girl continued, looking a little more sympathetic. "You'll probably be fine if you read through all those printouts that he just gave us and learn as much as possible off by heart. Mr. Buchen will give us all some training now. And I can give you a hand if you need it. I'm training to be a qualified wine expert, you see." She stuck out her hand. "I'm going to have my own winery one day. It's Madison, by the way. What's your name?"

"Belle," she replied, shaking the other woman's hand. "And thanks for that. Really appreciate it."

Madison gave a small smile and they followed the rest of the group to a small tasting lounge. There were several high tables in the middle of the room, each stocked with bottles of the Buchen Winery wines that would be served at the New Year's Eve party. Lines of glasses waited on a counter next to the tables.

Belle glanced at the bottles. They had gold embossed lettering printed on shiny black labels. She didn't have to taste them to know that they were expensive. In fact, she had already searched a little online before she came to work. A bottle of the Buchen sparkling white wine was ninety dollars alone!

"Maybe if I drink enough of this, I'll become a wine expert," she joked to Madison.

Madison frowned. "If you drink a lot of this, then you'll forget *anything* that you learn," she replied. "We just need to sample small amounts from them and know what the wine tastes like for tomorrow night. Fortunately, I already know about each of these vintages." She flashed a supercilious look at Belle. "So, unlike you, I'm going to have some free time tonight." She winked. "I plan to use it to get ready to enjoy the party with a special someone."

Just as Belle was going to ask the other woman more questions, their boss coughed for attention. "Ladies, gentlemen, sommeliers! Lend me your ears!" called Mr. Buchen from across the room. "Please proceed to educate yourselves about this year's wine menu."

Everyone proceeded to pour tiny amounts into wine glasses and to take small, thoughtful sips. A few held up the glasses to the light, swirling the contents.

Belle copied them, trying to work out what she was supposed to be looking for, while Mr. Buchen called out descriptions like "notes of raspberry and licorice", or "a hint of orange peel." Belle kept taking sips and trying to taste what he meant.

It all just tastes like alcohol to me.

"Don't swallow it," warned Madison, glancing at Belle, who was pulling a face after tasting one of the heavier red wines. "Have you been swallowing it? You need to spit it out into your spittoon, or you'll be completely drunk by the end of the afternoon."

Belle, already a little lightheaded, grinned. "Sure!"

Why not add spitting in public to my new skills?

She followed Madison's example, allowing the taste of whatever she had just sipped to linger in her mouth for a moment before spitting it out discreetly into her spittoon. Belle was infinitely thankful to Madison for telling her not to swallow every mouthful of wine. Given how quickly she had become light-headed, Belle had no doubt that she would otherwise have been completely wasted by the end of the afternoon.

"Mr. Buchen!" called Madison. "What do you think is the best wine on this list?"

He glanced at her thoughtfully for a moment and then checked off something on his clipboard. "The rosé," he replied, continuing to mark the sheet of paper in front of him. "It has notes of melon and lemon zest. It's definitely the most popular one with our clients, but it's not my personal favorite."

Madison wrote everything that he had said down on a separate sheet of paper. "What's your personal favorite, then?" she enquired.

"The Shiraz," he replied. "It has a lovely smooth finish and tastes like cherry with an aftertaste of cocoa."

Copying Madison, Belle wrote down the two descriptions too. She mouthed the words "cherry with an aftertaste of cocoa" to herself, praying that she would remember these descriptions off by heart when she was serving wine to party guests. Maybe if she mentioned these kinds of descriptions first, no one would ask her any questions.

The tasting went on for what felt like hours, but according to her watch it was only forty minutes. Finally, Mr. Buchen called an end to it and asked everyone to gather up their notes and go to the kitchen to study the different gourmet recipes that would be paired with the wine during a five-course round of appetizers and miniature servings of food. The Riesling would be served with pork medallions and the Moscato would be paired with a creamy pasta in small bowls. The Cabernet Franc would be served with samples of a rich cassoulet, a traditional French dish of white beans, sausage, and bacon.

"... and the Shiraz, my favorite, will be served with a deconstructed beef bourguignon," finished Mr. Buchen, pronouncing "bourguignon" in a French accent. "There's also cheese, crackers, and a dessert wine to study."

Belle had no idea how a beef bourguignon could possibly be deconstructed. She listened intently to everything Mr. Buchen said. But, after such a long morning, not much was sinking in.

She sighed and braced herself for a long night of study.

She knew that if she wanted to keep her job through to January, she had better get up to speed on wines before the New Year's Eve party the next day.

Chapter 3

The last day of the year dawned bright and clear, with sunlight streaming through Belle's window and waking her up. Belle yawned and stretched, opening one eye to peek at the clock.

It was nine o'clock.

She had several hours before she had to be at the Buchen winery to help set up for the evening's function. She snuggled deeper under the covers, her mind drifting to the night ahead. Last night's late-night studying had been hard work, but she'd managed to commit most of the Buchen wines to memory, as well as typical descriptors and the food that the wines would be paired with. The aromas "dark cherry, subtle chocolate and hint of spice" of the Shiraz and the "buttery notes of oak and hints of vanilla" of the Chardonnay were now firmly lodged in her memory. So firmly lodged that she had in fact been dreaming about them most of the night.

I just hope that it will be enough for tonight's New Year's Eve party!

Belle could hear her grandmother downstairs talking to Mittens. She allowed herself a few more minutes of lying in bed, before she started to feel guilty and made herself get up. Hopping into the shower, she quickly washed her hair and scrubbed herself with soap. It was not long before she was pulling on her tracksuit and heading downstairs to the kitchen where she knew her grandmother would already be busy.

"Morning Gram," Belle said, giving her a hug.

"Good morning, dear," her grandmother replied with a smile. "How did the studying go? You were up late. Thought that I would let you catch up on some sleep."

Belle nodded, stifling a yawn. "It was hard work, but I'm as ready as I'll ever be," she said, pouring herself a cup of coffee before sitting down at the table. "We only have a few last hours of the year to enjoy before I must head out to work. You know, I can't believe a whole year has passed again."

"That's what everyone says on New Year's Eve." Her grandmother chuckled as she washed a cup. "And that's why we all make New Year's resolutions. It is just a list of the things we didn't get to do during the year."

Belle gazed thoughtfully out of the kitchen window. The cottage garden was covered in a blanket of pristine white snow and glistened like sugar crystals.

What have I not got done this year?

As she pondered, movement caught her eye. She could see Mittens picking his way carefully across the lawn, chasing a fluttering snowflake back to the house. He loved chasing snowflakes.

Scraping her chair back from the breakfast table, Belle went to open the back door for her cat to come inside. A woosh of icy air rushed into the room as Mittens strolled in and meowed a friendly greeting. Belle quickly shut the door. "Brrr," she shivered. "You crazy cat! What are you doing outside?"

Grace came out of the pantry and wagged her finger at Mittens. "That cat of yours is always up to something," she said. Placing her hands on her hips, she looked pointedly at Belle. "He pulled off at least three decorations from the Christmas tree last night. I found them in his cat bed."

Belle chuckled, picking up her furball of a cat and cuddled him close. "He just loves Christmas, that's all."

Grace shook her head. "Well, Christmas is done, and we must now prepare for the New Year." She smiled at Belle. "So, what are your New Year's resolutions going to be this year?"

Belle thought for a moment, then smiled. "I'm going to try not to laugh too hard when Mittens gets himself into trouble," she said.

"That sounds like a resolution that will last five minutes." Grace stirred the breakfast oats. "Well, I will tell you what I am going to do. I'm going to try to eat more healthy and exercise more this year. And what about you, Mister?" She raised her eyebrows at Mittens. "Are you going to behave yourself?"

Mittens chirruped in a non-committal way.

Belle chuckled and then yawned again. "I haven't even had time to make any New Year's resolutions. This job has turned out to be a bit different to what I expected. I don't think that I will ever remember all of that stuff about wines," she said, putting Mittens down and taking a seat at the table again.

Grace tutt-tutted as she served up their breakfast into two bowls, added a dollop of cream, and sprinkled her special mixture of sugar, cinnamon, and nutmeg over the top. "Now, now. You'll be fine. You're taking this all much too seriously."

Belle shook her head, her long hair falling across her forehead. "But I want to do a good job so that Mr. Buchen will keep me on through January and maybe even hire me next year. He pays well for serving wines at this party, you know. Apparently, if you impress him, he remembers you and hires you again for the next event." She sipped her coffee.

Grace snorted. "It's just a party for rich people. I'm sure everyone will just be enjoying themselves."

Belle was no so sure, but she finished eating her breakfast quietly, enjoying the smell of cinnamon mixed with nutmeg.

After breakfast, her grandmother put their bowls to be washed and finished packing some sandwiches and some fresh cherries in a bag. "Here. This is for your lunch and dinner so that your blood sugar doesn't drop. Make sure that you eat properly. You need to keep your strength up, past midnight at least."

Belle smiled ruefully at the amount of food that her grandmother had packed. It was enough for two people! But she knew from experience that it was useless to object. "Thank you, Gram."

"So, will you have some time to have fun at the party, Belle?" Gram asked again with a twinkle in her eye.

Belle looked horrified. "Oh no, there is no time for that. I must be on my toes the whole time, delivering drinks and telling people about the Buchen wines. But who knows, maybe I'll get to see some famous people. That will be fun at least."

Her grandmother's face lit up. "That reminds me!" She hurried into the other room and returned with a magazine labeled 'Celebrity News'. "I got this from Doris. She collects them to see the latest fashions. Take this with you, and if you spot anyone important from it, take a picture! Maybe it will make the magazine!"

Belle laughed. "Gram, I'm not sure that's what Mr. Buchen hired me for." But she took the magazine anyway. The cover mentioned an article about hairstyles that looked interesting. "Thanks, Gram! I'm sure it will come in handy."

Grace winked. "You never know what might happen at a fancy party like this one," she said with a mischievous grin. "Maybe some rich bachelors?"

Belle rolled her eyes. "Gram, I'm sure there won't be any single rich bachelors wanting to date a server at a New Year's party out in the country."

Gram coughed. "You never know, my dear. You never know! And, if you don't have time to make a resolution, then I can help you out. My resolution for you is to make some memories and have some fun at the party. Now, will you help me sort out my end-of-year donations?"

Grace Beaumont had an "out with the old, in with the new" attitude towards New Year, that involved sorting through both of their wardrobes every year. They donated anything useful that they were not using to charity.

"Sure, I have a few hours free before I have to be at work," said Belle, resigning herself to a morning of cupboard sorting.

A few hours later, Belle and her grandmother had filled several bags of clothes for charity and Belle was free to change into her server's outfit of black pants, a shirt and a neat black jacket. Pulling on a pair of comfortable boots, her thick winter jacket and knitted scarf, she grabbed her notes on the Buchen wines and packed her sandwiches in her bag before leaving for the long drive to work.

An hour or so later, she was crunching through the powdered snow on the winery's driveway, marveling at the picture-perfect scene before her.

The vineyards were covered in snow and the air was crisp. Fairy lights were strung up along the entrance to a large white marquee where the party would be held. It looked like a semi-permanent building with special flooring laid down and several gas heaters warming the inside. People dressed in black uniforms were already at work, carrying music equipment to the temporary stage on the other side of the marquee. The scent of cooking onions and baking bread wafted in the air, and she could see people unloading crates of wine glasses. Several servers were organizing bar tables and gas heaters.

Belle checked her watch. She had a few minutes before the pre-party meeting for the servers.

She quickly put her packed food in the small staff fridge in the kitchen and hurried to the staff room in the main building to visit the restroom. She checked that her long chestnut hair was still tightly scraped back into its ponytail. Then, grabbing her notes, she headed to the tasting room where everyone had gathered before the big night.

Madison was already there, talking to some of the other servers. Her thick auburn hair was styled in a sophisticated chignon and she wore a black cocktail dress, simple in cut but appealing. Her shoes looked like they had cost a fortune.

"You look great, Madison!" said Belle. "Aren't you cold?"

"I'm trying to make an impression," she replied, with a slight smile. "This is my career, after all." She looked at Belle's outfit, her face falling somewhat. "And you look lovely, too," she added, politely.

Belle glanced down at her sensible black shirt and pants and couldn't help but feel a little drab. The pants fitted well, but they were blocky, and her shirt suddenly felt like something that a schoolgirl would have worn. Belle self-consciously pulled her plain black jacket closer. After sorting through her wardrobe earlier, she was well aware that she did not own anything like Madison's dress.

It's better to wear something warm than something pretty.

Mr. Buchen came in then, to brief the serving team on their duties for the night. Belle tried to dismiss her worries about her outfit from her mind as her boss updated everyone what was happening in the kitchen and the stock levels of the Buchen wines. She clutched her notes and listened intently, taking it all in with determination.

"… and that's it," Mr. Buchen concluded with an efficient smile. "Any questions?"

She breathed deeply and shook her head, along with everyone else who seemed to know what they needed to do. The other servers moved off to prepare their stations. Belle stood about indecisively for a moment.

"Belle! Come help us set up!" said one of the other wine servers, a guy called Tyler. "We need more wine decanters. Then you can stand with us while the guests arrive."

Relieved that she did not have to stand next to Madison in her elegant dress, Belle was more than happy to have something to do. She turned to join the others in laying out the glassware, while a live band set up on the small stage. "Coming!"

Chapter 4

After the glassware had been stacked on the wine-tasting tables, Belle had just enough time to look through her notes once more before someone mentioned that the guests had started arriving. She grabbed the magazine that Gram had given her and hid it in her jacket.

All the servers picked up their trays of the different drinks that they were each assigned to serve and hurried to their positions outside the entrance of the marquee. A limousine pulled up and a man wearing sunglasses and a tuxedo stepped out. He was followed by a glamorous couple, their faux-fur coats shimmering in the winter light. Another car arrived behind them, and two actresses stepped out, their long gowns trailing behind them on the snow, as they made their way into the marquee.

The party had started!

Belle watched in awe as the rich and famous descended on the Buchen Winery, their chauffeured cars dropping them at the entrance to the winery and driving away to park somewhere and wait. The women wore expensive long dresses, pearls, and jewels; and the tuxedoed men looked like flocking birds migrating for the season.

"Is that...?" whispered Belle to Tyler, trying not to point, as a tall, slim woman stepped out of the back seat of a luxury car. She looked very much like the famous singer, who was featured in her grandmother's gossip magazine.

Tyler smiled knowingly and nodded. "And there are some actors from that well-known drama show here tonight too. Do you watch 'As the Day Turns?'"

Belle shook her head.

"Oh well, they are very famous," replied the server, watching the guests now walking into the winery.

Belle tried her best not to be too obviously starstruck, but the people around her didn't seem to mind. After a while, Belle realized that Madison had been standing next to her for some time, watching the arrivals with an expression of admiration and envy.

"It looks like they've got it all, doesn't it?" Madison said in a low voice.

Belle nodded and watched as the guests made their way into the marquee, sampling the wines and chatting casually. "It sure does. But you never know. Money and fame don't always make people happy," Belle said thoughtfully. "Living a good and happy life is more important."

Madison looked at Belle with pity. "That's exactly what people say who don't have any money or any fame."

Belle didn't know what to say to that, and they stood quietly while the next car drove up to the entrance.

"Who do you think that is?" said Belle, nodding at the new arrival and nudging Madison's arm in excitement.

A woman had just stepped out of the limousine, dressed up in a bold red dress with gold accents. The dress contrasted against the snow like a flame. Her strappy heels looked like something that you would wear to a beach, not a New Year's Eve party in an outside marquee. But then again, Mr. Buchen had insisted on making the closed marquee as comfortable as possible for the event and it was quite warm inside.

"Oh, I don't know. Some business tycoon's wife," said Madison distractedly. Her eyes wandered around the arriving guests as if she were looking for someone.

Belle looked back at the woman in the red dress. Her hair was done up in an elegant bun, which showed off her long neck. She took the arm of an older-looking man in a tuxedo, and the couple headed inside.

"Actually, I think that she's a famous actress," said Belle after they had passed. She rested her tray on a table for a moment and quickly paged through her magazine until she reached the article about current hairstyles.

"I think her name is Gina, something or other." She showed the article to Madison. "She must be freezing in that dress."

"Whatever. We had better get back to our stations," said Madison, without glancing at the magazine, "or we'll be in trouble with Mr. Buchen." She sniffed and adjusted her dress before setting off into the crowd, her tray held up high.

Belle nodded, feeling a little silly for being so excited to see famous people. She followed the other woman as they slipped through the crowd to their serving stations.

The band had already started playing live jazz music. Belle looked around the room with interest. She didn't recognize any other famous faces, and everyone looked pretty much like normal people would, except that they were wearing expensive clothes and the women were wearing sparkling jewelry. Tyler had told her that the party attracted the Hollywood scene as well as successful business people. There were certainly a lot of people taking selfies of themselves with their phones. Belle guessed that they were the social media influencers. All of them looked sufficiently wealthy to pay the large entry fee.

Waitresses and waiters circulated the room with trays of very expensive hors d'oeuvres. The staff had been strictly informed that they were not to eat any, but Belle had seen a couple of servers sneaking a few gourmet pastries when no one was looking. She had not been brave enough to do the same yet. Not that she cared. She wasn't a big fan of oysters and had no desire to try caviar.

Various wine stations had been set up along the length of the marquee, each serving a few vintages of a specific wine. Belle's wine station was at the very end of the area, near the doors to the gardens, doors that were currently closed tight against the cold. She would be serving three kinds of champagne: a Méthode Traditionnelle, a Blanc de Noir, and a Rosé. Belle remembered that they had notes of peach, raspberry, and rose, respectively. She felt better about serving champagne now that she knew what it was.

By the time that Belle had reached her station, four well-dressed guests were already waiting, talking animatedly about some Hollywood film project. Belle quickly poured out a few glasses of the rosé champagne and set them onto a coaster in front of the guests, thankfully without spilling anything on their clothes or shoes.

She smiled as she handed out the glasses, hoping that her nerves would abate as the evening wore on. From where Belle's wine station was located, halfway down the large room, she could see Madison through the crowd, her auburn hair catching the light. Madison was in charge of one of the popular red wine stations, serving four vintages of red wine: a Pinot Noir, a Zweigelt, a Cabernet, and a Merlot. The other server was laughing gracefully, men in tuxedos standing about the station like so many black and white moths attracted to a flame.

Belle looked around her own little wine station. It wasn't even busy yet. Hoping that she wouldn't need to look as confident as Madison, she repeated the names and descriptions of the sparkling wines to herself so she wouldn't forget them.

Waiters threaded their way through the arriving crowd with trays of water and canapés.

Suddenly, Mr. Buchen's voice boomed loudly over the hubbub of the arriving crowd. "I would like to welcome all of you to our New Year's Eve celebrations." Everyone applauded politely as Mr. Buchen looked around the room with a broad smile. "Please circulate around to each of the tasting stations and see what you think about our world-famous wines. The firework display will begin shortly. We wish you a Happy New Year's and... enjoy yourself!" He beamed with pride as everyone applauded again, and the band started up with a livelier version of their jazzy songs.

Belle looked up as a couple of guests approached her wine station. She smiled politely and poured fizzing champagne into flutes for them.

Before long, a few sharp bursts outside heralded the start of the firework display, and soon the night sky was filled with bright sparks and showers of color. The party guests were able to see everything through the clear windows of the marquee, although some of them braved the cold to go out and take in the spectacle outside. Inside the warm marquee, everyone cheered as each new pattern exploded in a kaleidoscope of light.

Suddenly, out of the corner of her eye, she noticed Madison leaving her station and heading to a door that led out into the gardens, laughing and looking flirtatiously back at a man in a tuxedo, who followed her.

Was Madison leaving her post?

They had strict instructions not to leave their wine serving stations during the evening, except for restroom breaks, and to fetch more glassware or wine bottles from the cellar.

Belle wondered whether Madison needed to go to the cellar for more wine already. She tried to focus as she poured the Blanc de Noir for more guests, repeating by rote what she had learned about that particular vintage. They swirled the bubbly wine in their glasses and took elegant sips, while Belle kept looking at Madison's wine station.

It was still unmanned.

The first part of the firework display lasted about twenty minutes and Belle concentrated on pouring some of the Méthode Traditionnelle champagne into fresh glasses for the guests, while glancing about for her co-worker. There were already a few people gathering about Madison's station, waiting to be served. Hopefully, Mr. Buchen hadn't seen Madison leave, or the woman would soon be in big trouble.

Eventually, the guests hanging about Belle's station wandered off to speak to a glamorous group of people on the other side of the room.

Belle wondered whether she should dash over to Madison's station and pour wine for the people waiting there until the auburn-haired woman returned. But then Belle didn't know about any of the wines Madison was serving. It was difficult enough to have memorized the information about the three champagnes at her own station, and some of the other white wines, as well as the history of the Buchen Winery, in case anyone asked.

Where on earth had Madison disappeared to?

Belle chewed her lip, as she weighed up what to do. While she was focused on an internal debate, a voice spoke nearby, "Excuse me, but could I trouble you for a glass?"

She jumped and turned to see a quiet-looking fellow in glasses. He was thin and serious, not at all the type of guest she had expected to see at this event. He was wearing an ill-fitting tuxedo that was very much out of place amongst the well-dressed crowd.

She immediately pinned her professional smile on her face. "Oh, yes. Of course."

He thanked her and turned his head to watch the crowd sway in time to the music. The band had started playing a new set of songs, and the guests seemed to be enjoying themselves.

"We're having quite a party, aren't we?" he added neutrally, after they had both watched for a moment.

"Well, I'm working, but it looks like they're having a good time," she said cheerfully, handing him a glass of champagne.

"Ah, yes, the rich and famous," he said, flatly. "With more money than they know what to do with."

Belle wasn't sure what to make of this guy, but she had no time to worry about it because she had just spotted Mr. Buchen standing near Madison's unmanned wine station, looking around. Her boss's face was scrunched up in a frown, and she could immediately tell that he was searching for Madison.

Just as Belle was wondering how she could possibly cover for her co-worker, Madison reappeared. She was carrying a couple of dusty bottles of wine, as if she had been to the cellar in the main building. The girl smiled at Mr. Buchen and the crowd around her and continued to pour drinks as if nothing had happened. Her face looked a little flushed, but other than that she seemed normal.

Belle frowned. She was certain that Madison had left the ballroom through one door leading to the garden and that she had left with a man. But she had returned through the main doors as if from the main building.

Maybe I was mistaken.

Belle shook her head to clear it. By this time, the man in the ill-fitting tuxedo had moved off into the growing crowd.

She stifled a yawn and glanced at her watch, as the band struck up a new tune. It was ten o'clock.

"This is going to be a very long night," she sighed.

Chapter 5

"Belle, is that you?" a familiar voice spoke.

Belle turned in surprise.

A plump brunette in her sixties stood before her, in a bright purple dress that did nothing for her complexion, with a plunging neckline that showed off an impressive amount of cleavage.

It was Wilma, the President of the local Women's Guild.

Belle automatically poured her a glass of champagne. "It has notes of citrus and pear," she said by rote, as she slid the champagne flute across the little counter. "What on earth are you doing here, Wilma?" she said in a low voice, looking around. "This is an invitation-only event."

Wilma leaned forward and shot Belle an arched look before whispering, "I got an invitation! Can you believe it? Buchen Winery gave three free tickets to the Town Council, so that we could send the mayor and a couple of other important people. I forget who." She waved a dismissive hand. "One of them couldn't make it, so here I am!"

Belle closed her mouth that must have been hanging open. Wilma was well known in Cherryville for organizing, or perhaps rather mis-organizing, the town's fundraisers. She was also one of the town's biggest social climbers.

"I hope that you aren't asking people here to come to your next fundraiser. They aren't the sort of crowd to appreciate a quilting bee," Belle said, meaningfully, as she held out the glass of champagne.

"I won't say no to a free drink," Wilma replied, taking the glass and inspecting it closely, then taking a long sip.

Is she checking that the glassware is clean?

"Plus, these people are *exactly* the kind of people that we need to invite to our town's fundraisers," continued Wilma, shooting Belle an appraising look after tasting the champagne. "Good heavens, what an upgrade for you from the hot chocolate booth!" She winked.

Wilma hadn't forgotten that Belle had worked the hot chocolate booth at Harvey's Christmas Tree Farm over Christmas. The previous year, Harvey had let the local Women's Guild, headed by Wilma, take control of the hot chocolate booth. Unfortunately, not only had the hot chocolate recipe been reworked by Wilma until it was almost undrinkable, but the Women's Guild had been so enthusiastic that they had scared off most of Harvey's customers. After that debacle, Harvey had refused to ask them to run the booth again and Wilma wasn't one to forget such things quickly.

"At least this place is indoors!" Wilma gave Belle another meaningful wink and then moved off to mingle with other guests, thankfully disappearing into the crowd.

The woman had an almost supernatural ability to socially elevate herself.

However, Belle didn't have long to wonder about Wilma's antics. The party had fast become quite crowded, and she was soon run off her feet. A few people asked her questions about the wine, and Belle parroted what she had learned from her notes, sufficient to make herself sound educated. However, it turned out that most of the guests weren't really interested in learning about the wine. People seemed to just want to drink it like soda and to dance to the music played by the band.

All that stressing about memorizing the fancy wines that were served had been for nothing!

A few servers circulated with trays piled high with food. The chorizo-stuffed dates topped with almonds looked amazing, as did the scallops wrapped in prosciutto and the little mini quiches.

The last display of fireworks before midnight had started and showers of colored sparks lit up the sky again over the vineyard. Many of the guests stood watching the display and Belle took the opportunity to rest for a moment. Her feet had started to ache, so she dragged a stool behind her counter and sat on it. She checked her watch again.

Eleven-forty-five! Would this night never end?

Suddenly, a tall man with dark hair and brown eyes approached her station and leaned against it. He looked like a young Pierce Brosnan, all debonaire and suave. "Tough night?" he said in a deep voice.

"Oh, hello!" she replied, a little startled and jumping to her feet. "Could I offer you some of the champagne? It's got notes of pear and citrus," she said.

"Sure," said the dark-haired man, sitting on a stool near her counter. "I haven't seen you here before."

Belle smiled in surprise. "I'm new," she replied. "Do you come here often?"

"Well, we're lucky that you happened along then," he said, refraining from answering her question. "This party is usually so stuffy. You should drink one too."

"Oh no. I shouldn't really," replied Belle, politely, uncorking a new bottle. "I just serve the champagne."

It turned out to be a good decision, because just then, Mr. Buchen appeared at her elbow.

"Please make sure you serve all the *paying* customers, Belle," he said sharply, giving the dark-haired guest a hard look. He turned and rearranged some of the glasses on Belle's counter in straight lines.

"Yes, sir," answered Belle, immediately, unsure what he had meant. All of the guests had bought tickets to attend, as far as she knew.

Mr. Buchen nodded once, gave the other man an unsmiling look for a moment too long, and then moved over to check on the next table.

"Geez, what a stuffed shirt," said the handsome stranger, as soon as Mr. Buchen had left. He rolled his eyes and pulled a comical face.

Belle giggled. "He's okay."

He leaned over, took the bottle off her and grabbed two champagne flutes from the neatly arranged glassware on the counter. "Let's mess up the straight lines here," he grinned, and poured two glasses. He held out one glass for her to take. "Come on, it's about to be midnight and no one will know." He held her gaze for a moment too long. Belle had the oddest feeling that she knew him from somewhere, but couldn't place where she may have seen him before.

She glanced about for Mr. Buchen, but he was nowhere to be seen. There were no more customers at her station.

"Oh, go on," he said, widening his eyes. "Live a little."

Perhaps it was the music or the fact that a handsome man had chosen to flirt with her, but before she knew it, a spirit of rebellion rose in her chest.

What was she? Cinderella?

"Oh, why not? It's nearly midnight, after all" she said, taking the glass and chinking it against his. "Cheers!"

"That's right," he said, smiling. "Parties are much more fun when you have a gorgeous girl to flirt with."

Belle blushed. "Well, I'm sure you're making many other ladies at the party happy," she said, grinning at him cheekily.

It was fun to feel part of the party for a minute, rather than just a servant at a ball. Belle relaxed a little and she found herself laughing again at the man's "stuffed shirt" comment and how he had messed with the neatly ordered champagne flutes on the counter. Mr. Buchen did indeed look like he ironed his shirts a little too much.

She took another sip of champagne. Suddenly, a feeling of being watched made her turn her head. She looked around and found Madison frowning at her from across the room.

The man spoke again, "I wonder, would you like to dance with me?" His smile was hard to resist as he held out his free hand, the other still holding his champagne glass. "We only have a few minutes before midnight."

Belle looked at him. She glanced back around for Madison, but she had disappeared into the crowd. "I should really work."

"Work is for tomorrow. You have a whole year of work ahead of you," he said, taking her hand and linking arms with her. "Come on, let's go dance." He led her inexorably to the dance floor.

"Okay. Why not?" she said, giving in, the champagne making her feel all warm inside. The drab Belle of black pants and sensible shirt was forgotten!

The band had started up a pop favorite, and the handsome man took her into the middle of the dance floor and twirled her around, all without spilling his drink.

Belle laughed as she spun around. She had not been out dancing for ages. "Oh, this is such fun!" she exclaimed, as they weaved their way about the packed dance floor.

The dance floor was crowded and in no time, her dancing partner bumped shoulders with someone. The other man turned, and Belle recognized him as the uninterested fellow who had visited her wine station earlier that evening. He frowned at both of them.

Belle's handsome partner pulled another comical face and wagged his finger at the other man, who turned away and disappeared into the crowd.

"Who was that?" asked Belle, out of breath from dancing.

"Someone who isn't thrilled to see me here," he replied briefly, taking her hand and dancing a few steps of the Charleston.

Belle found herself swept up in the throng of people, as the countdown to midnight began. Some partygoers near her were counting down, "Ten... nine... eight..."

A cheer went up from the room as a ball, covered in Christmas lights, began its descent from the ceiling. Belle laughed and clapped her hands. She looked around for Madison and wondered why her co-worker had been frowning. However, by now, Belle was feeling quite tipsy and wasn't sure if she had just imagined Madison's behavior.

Who cares? She had a handsome stranger who wanted to dance with her and made her heart beat faster! This party wasn't so bad, after all.

"Hey! Are you okay?" said the man, taking Belle's hand and looking at her curiously.

She nodded and joined the chanting as they counted down to midnight. The room was filled with people shouting and laughing. "Three... two... one!"

"Happy New Year!" cried everyone around her, as fireworks lit up the night sky and the band struck up "Auld Lang Syne." The crowd surged together, hugging and kissing. Belle looked up at her handsome new friend, who suddenly pressed his lips against hers.

After a momentary surprise, the champagne coursing through Belle's veins threw caution to the wind. Before she knew what she was doing, Belle found her lips returning the stranger's kiss for a moment before breaking away.

"Happy New Year, Belle!" he said, smiling in a debonaire way like a model in a Vogue magazine.

"Happy New Year, yourself!" she repeated, shaking her head and laughing.

Just for a moment, Belle was happy to forget about medical bills, or learning about wines, or finding another job next year. As everyone cheered the New Year in, for a moment, Belle let herself just relax and dance to the beat of the music.

Chapter 6

The party roared on in the marquee, as Belle helped the other servers pack up for the night. After her momentary celebration at midnight, Belle had returned to her post at her wine station and stayed there, working away while the other servers finished up serving all of their wine stock. The handsome man, who had been flirting with her when the ball dropped, had mysteriously disappeared soon after. Belle was a little disappointed that he hadn't at least said goodbye. Now that the brief euphoria of the champagne had cleared from her brain, she realized that the handsome stranger was probably just a chronic flirt.

Now, even though it was past midnight, several guests were still dancing, drinking, and eating. The band was going strong on stage, belting out their set of the night. The three musicians on stage looked like they were still full of life and energy, while Belle felt like she had run a marathon. She checked her watch. It was one o'clock in the morning.

I have been on my feet for eight hours nonstop.

Belle was exhausted, but she couldn't head home until they had carried all the used wine glasses into the kitchen in the main building and cleaned up the wine station area. Several glasses had been broken in the festivities, and Belle spent some time sweeping up broken glass before anyone stood on it. She was finishing up, when Madison pushed past her.

"Happy New Year, Madison!" said Belle, grinning. "Thank you so much for your help learning about wines. It all worked out okay in the end. But I don't think that I could have done it without you."

"Yeah, right," snapped Madison. "Don't let your success go to your head. You still have a lot of lessons to learn. And I won't always be around to help."

Belle stared back at her in shock.

Madison stalked out of the marquee and over to the main building, muttering angrily. Belle heard a phone ring and saw Madison put it to her ear. She made some angry gestures, as if the person she was calling was not answering.

Why was Madison upset with her?

Belle didn't have time to wonder any further as just then, Mr. Buchen called all of them out to the main building and into the kitchen to thank them for their help. As the staff gathered, it didn't surprise Belle to see that Madison stayed well away from her, barely acknowledging Belle's presence with a sullen grunt.

"I'd like to thank everyone for their help tonight," said Mr. Buchen. "You did a great job and I'm very pleased with your efforts."

Everyone clapped, relieved that the night had gone so well. They chattered about how much money they had made that night in tips, and what they would do with it. However, Belle wasn't interested in hearing about how some of the younger waiters were saving up for a car. She was more interested in getting home and curling up in bed. It would still be an hour's drive and she would have to drive carefully on the snow-banked roads. She slid her pay into her pocket.

"And remember that you're all hired to help with the Spring Ball in April, so I'll see the casual workers again then!" said Mr. Buchen cheerfully. Amazingly, his tuxedo was uncreased and still looked like it was freshly pressed. "Don't forget all you've learned about our wines. For the rest of you who are working through January, you'll have tomorrow off, and then it's back to work."

Everyone dispersed, chattering amongst themselves. The sound of the dishwashing machines reverberated against the kitchen walls, as the kitchen staff finished cleaning the glassware.

Belle nudged Tyler. "April?" she said, surprised, "And that is an automatic hire? We don't have to be interviewed again or anything?"

"Nope," he said dryly, "I've been here every year, since I turned eighteen. I have a permanent spot at the wine bar in the main building."

He gave her a wink. "Looks like you learned your stuff quickly enough for the boss to let you stay."

"Really? That's great!" April was several months off, but she would make sure she was available for the Spring Ball. It was worth it for the money that Mr. Buchen had just paid each of them. Plus, she would work at the winery throughout January and could count on a month's worth of pay.

Thank goodness! She had a job for January and for later in April!

She would be able to pay for the next instalment owing on her grandmother's medical bills. She may even be able to afford a new pair of boots.

It had been an exciting night, and she smiled as she remembered celebrating the New Year with a handsome stranger. At least it was a splendid memory to start the year with.

She headed to the staff room to gather her bag. Pushing her tired arms into her coat, she picked up her bag, then headed back down the hallway and past the kitchen.

Suddenly, a scream cut through the frosty night air. Everyone in the kitchen stood stock-still in dead silence.

"Help!" someone shouted. "Call the hospital!"

"What on earth?" asked Mr. Buchen, turning toward the noise, as a server came running in.

Tyler was panting like he had ran up the stairs, and his buzz-cut seemed to stand on end even more than usual.

"There's a guy collapsed in the restroom!" he shouted. "I think that he's dead!" The poor fellow looked ashen. "I went in there to wash my hands and I saw him facedown on the floor."

"Who is lying on the floor?" said Mr. Buchen, frowning. "Is there someone in the restroom?"

"Yes, a guy has collapsed on the floor," repeated the server, panicking.

"Someone has called the paramedics already," said one of the other servers, coming into the kitchen behind them. "The ambulance should be here soon, the dispatcher said."

The room erupted into chaos as everyone started talking and shouting at the same time. Belle hurried as fast as she could with the buzz-cut waiter, Tyler, toward the restroom, as Mr. Buchen tried to calm everyone down and find out what was going on.

Tyler pushed open the door of the men's restroom and she immediately saw a man in a tuxedo lying on the floor near the sink. His face was turned to look at the wall. The black of the man's jacket was a stark contrast to the expensive white marble tiles, like a fallen crow on snow.

Belle's heart jumped into her throat, as she leaned down, hoping that he was still alive. She pressed her fingers against his neck where she imagined his pulse would be, but couldn't feel anything.

"I don't think he's breathing," whispered one server, peering over Belle's shoulder at the lifeless body lying face-down on the floor. He turned away, horrified.

"Don't touch him!" shouted Madison, who had appeared behind Belle. "He's probably just drunk. We should leave him alone!" Then, she gasped at the sight of the fellow lying on the floor.

"What?" said Belle. "You don't know that! He might need CPR."

"I think she's right," said Tyler as he pulled her away from the prone man figure. "We'll let the paramedics do their thing when they arrive."

Mr. Buchen came in to check on them, his face pale but his voice was steady. "What's happening?" he asked.

"We don't know," said Tyler, shaking his head. "He hasn't moved and we haven't touched him. The ambulance is on its way."

"I'll go out and meet it," said Mr. Buchen, who clearly didn't enjoy being involved in a medical emergency. He left the room quickly.

Everyone continued to stare at the man on the floor, who lay very still.

"Does anyone know any first-aid?" asked Belle, desperately. She dimly remembered the first aid course she had completed when helping at a scouts' camp. "Can anyone do CPR?"

Everyone just stood around helplessly. Fortunately, the paramedics had pulled up outside in their ambulance and were already hurrying in with their medical supplies.

"Where is the patient?" the first paramedic demanded, pushing his way through the crowd that had formed outside of the men's restroom.

"In there," said a server bluntly, pointing. "I think he drank too much and may have had an alcohol or drug overdose."

"Or maybe he hit his head on the basin," said another of the onlookers, a woman in a ballgown. "He might have been knocked out and crawled in here to sleep it off."

"You shouldn't all be standing here," said the paramedic in a loud voice. "Can you please clear the room so that we can do our job?"

They all stood back to let the paramedics get to the body of the unfortunate man. They worked on him for a few minutes, but he it looked like he hadn't been breathing for some time.

Everyone stood around in shocked silence.

"I'm sorry, there's nothing that we can do," said the other paramedic, after checking over the man more thoroughly. "It's too late."

The crowd outside gasped. There were comments about a famous playboy who may have taken drugs.

Belle felt sick to her stomach, as she watched the paramedics cover the poor man with a sheet. As the crowd parted, she caught a glimpse of his face under a thick wave of brown hair. She recognized him instantly.

It was the man who had been flirting with her! The one she had been dancing with at midnight and who had given her a cheeky kiss.

"Oh my gosh, I know that guy!" she gasped.

A wave of nausea rushed over her. Horrible memories of having seen another dead body just weeks ago flooded back.

"I'm sure you do," said Madison angrily. Her auburn hair seemed to curl with anger, as she turned to the paramedics. "I saw her dancing with him in the ballroom earlier," she added, pointing at Belle. "She spent the evening with him."

Chapter 7

"Belle, are you awake?" said Grace, peeping around the bedroom door, as Belle opened one eye.

"I'm awake," Belle replied groggily. She sat up in bed and rubbed her eyes. "Although, don't come near me. I must be the world's worst bad luck charm."

"Happy New Year, dear. I've made us a nice cup of tea." Grace was still standing by the door, looking at Belle anxiously. "You look like you could do with one. Why don't you get dressed and come downstairs? I'll put some toast on."

It was New Year's Day, the day after the party. After the paramedics had eventually left, Belle had driven home in a bit of a daze, trying to concentrate on not driving too fast on the snow-covered roads. It was about three o'clock in the morning by the time she had tiptoed into the cottage as quietly as she could, trying not to wake Gram. She had pulled on her pajamas and brushed her teeth. Then, she had fallen into bed and almost immediately fallen asleep. She glanced at the clock. That was less than four hours ago.

"Hang on," Belle said, as she continued to eye the clock. "It's still early. Why don't you give me a few more minutes." She closed her eyes and lay down again.

I need to recover from helping discover yet another dead person.

"Umm, the thing is that Sheriff Barnes is here to ask you questions." Grace stuck her head back around the door, eyebrows raised. "He won't say what it's about. It must have been quite a party at the winery last night." Her face was agog with curiosity.

That was enough to wake Belle up completely. The events of the night before came rushing back in technicolor. The twinkling fairy lights, the jazz band, the expensive dresses, the fancy wine, and the dead body of the guy who had kissed her at midnight. Suddenly, her head pounded.

"Sheriff Barnes is here? Why?" She sat up straight again.

Mittens, who had been sleeping peacefully on the end of the bed, jumped up at the movement and padded out of the room. "Fine. I'll get dressed and come downstairs. Gram, can you make some toast for me? I'll be down as soon as I can."

"Of course," said Grace, looking at her with a frown. "What's going on?"

"You won't believe it when I tell you," Belle said. "Let me get some clothes on first."

Her grandmother huffed with impatience and hurried off to make the promised tea and toast.

Belle quickly pulled on her jeans and a jumper and brushed her hair back into a ponytail, tying it with an elastic band that she found in her pocket.

Rushing downstairs, Mittens at her heels, Belle saw Sheriff Barnes talking to Grace in the kitchen.

"Good morning, Belle," he said, giving her a nod. "I hope that you don't mind me taking up your time like this on New Year's Day, but I need to ask you some questions about last night."

"Of course, Sheriff Barnes. You're just doing your job," she replied. She crossed the room and sat down at the large table, where Grace had put out mugs, milk, and sugar. "Tea for me too, please, Gram."

"Yes, please," said Sheriff Barnes, ensconcing himself at the kitchen table, as Grace placed a plate of freshly baked bread on the table together with butter and strawberry jam. He drew his eyes away from the fresh loaf with difficulty and turned to Belle. "I believe that you knew the gentleman who died?"

"So, someone died?" Grace interrupted his line of questioning, her hand on her chest. "What? Another person?"

For a town where hardly anything happened, this was the second suspicious death that had happened in a month.

"Yes, Gram," answered Belle, quickly filling her in on the events of the night before. "He was a guest, but I'm afraid that he never told me his name."

"An unfortunate thing to have happened," said Sheriff Barnes firmly. "He was found in the men's restroom, collapsed on the floor. The man who died was Reginald Hartford."

"Hartford," muttered Belle thoughtfully. The name seemed familiar somehow. "I think I've heard of him."

"You may have. He's quite a celebrity around these parts. No one knows much about him, apart from the fact that he's quite rich and sometimes drives around in his luxury Porsche."

"Are you talking about Reginald Hartford, the billionaire?" said Grace, her eyes round. "The one who's always featured in the local gossip magazines?" She jerked her thumb over her shoulder in the direction of the pile of magazines that she had collected in the living room and that she liked to look at several times before throwing them away. "What a handsome man he is! Just like a movie star."

"Yes, that's him," said Sheriff Barnes. He turned to Belle. "Or that *was* him, I should say. You were there when his body was discovered, Belle. I need you to tell me everything you know. Leave nothing out. I've been called in to help the police in that county. They're short-staffed over Christmas."

Belle sighed and described exactly what had happened that night, from when she was dancing with Reginald to when Tyler came running in to tell them to call emergency services. She listed all the people whom she remembered being at the party, including Wilma from the Women's Guild. The only part in the story that she left out was the part where Reginald had kissed her. It wasn't exactly something that she wanted to tell the police.

"Well, I never!" exclaimed Grace, proud as punch. "Reginald Hartford flirting with you. Who would've thought it?"

"He was definitely flirting with me, but he said nothing about himself, not even his name. And then he disappeared soon after midnight."

"That will be enough for now," interjected Sheriff Barnes. "The medical examiner is working on establishing Mr. Hartford's cause of death. Could you please come to the station later? I'll most likely need to ask you a few more questions, as further information comes to light."

"Of course, Sheriff Barnes. You can ask me anything you want."

Grace offered the policeman some fresh bread, butter, and strawberry jam. "I can toast it for you, if you like," she said.

"Thank you, that would be lovely."

As the sheriff munched his toast, Belle wondered if her grandmother's baking was the only reason that he had come to ask her questions. Belle focused on sipping her tea and trying to wake up before eating anything.

When Sheriff Barnes left, Grace closed the front door and came back into the kitchen. "Good heavens," she said. "I can't believe it."

"Neither can I, Gram," said Belle. "But you never know. I assume that he died of natural causes. Or possibly a drug overdose. That was what they were saying last night." She bit into her bread and jam hungrily. It was delicious, warm and soft, with just the right amount of butter.

Her grandmother frowned. "Now, tell me again exactly what happened last night."

After Belle had gone through the events of the previous night a second time, Gram called her friend Doris. "She may know what happened."

Belle let her go ahead. There was no stopping the rumor mill now. If there was one thing Cherryville was good at, it was gossiping.

"It was murder," said Doris when she answered Gram's call. "He looked too healthy to die of natural causes. In fact, he looked as healthy as an ox in all the photos in those magazines. But they could have been photoshopped, you know."

"Yes, I know." Grace put her new mobile phone on FaceTime. She had just discovered how to use FaceTime and now she wanted to use it for every call. "Belle was there when they found him."

"Oh, my goodness!" said Doris, her ear close to the screen. "Why didn't you say so? What happened?"

"You've got to hold the screen to your face, Doris. Not your ear," Gram explained to her friend how the technology worked.

Doris' face suddenly appeared very close to the screen. "Like this?" she shouted.

"Yes, although, we can hear you fine," answered Gram. "Now, Belle, you tell Doris exactly what happened."

Knowing that she would get no peace until she did so, Belle took a deep breath and repeated her story. This time, she left out the minor detail of Reginald flirting with her, choosing instead to focus on the important parts. She told Doris that Reginald had fallen down in the men's restroom and died, but never mentioned how she had danced with him, or any of his flirty comments, or the fact that he had kissed her at midnight. That wasn't something she wanted to add to the rumors going around town.

"He must have been murdered," repeated Doris firmly, when Belle was done. "A young man doesn't just fall over and die next to a toilet, all on his own."

"The medical examiner will tell us whether it was natural causes," said Gram, with all the confidence of someone who regularly watches police detective TV shows. "Unfortunate thing to happen at a party."

Doris agreed, her voice full of suspicion, "Isn't it, though?"

Belle let the two old ladies natter to each other about the events of the previous night, while she fixed herself some coffee. She was too tired to join in the chatter. She yawned widely as she waited for the coffee to brew, its rich, earthy scent helping her tired morning headache. Just the smell of the coffee was making her feel better.

"But I have to tell you something, Doris, you'll never guess," said Gram, lowering her voice to a whisper. "Wilma was there too, in a ballgown and everything!"

"No!" cried Doris, her voice cracking with disbelief. "How on earth did she get an invitation?"

"I don't know, but she was there. Belle saw her, didn't you, my dear?"

Belle rolled her eyes at Gram's phone screen. "Yes, she was there."

"Well, there you go then. Straight from the mouth of an eyewitness."

Belle shook her head.

Who would have thought the fact that Wilma, the self-important President of the Women's Guild, had attended the New Year's Eve Party at the Buchen Winery, would be bigger news than the death of a playboy billionaire?

Chapter 8

Cherryville was quiet at midday on New Year's Day, with everyone sleeping off their hangovers. It had rained, and the snow was turning to slush. There were very few cars out and about, as Belle drove her old station wagon into town.

Her mind was still buzzing with everything that had happened over the last twenty-four hours. As much as she felt bad for Reginald and his family, she couldn't help but feel a little sorry for herself, too.

What are the chances that I'm right there to help find another body? What bad luck that the first and only handsome billionaire who flirts with me winds up dead?

Belle grumbled to herself as she pulled into a parking space in front of the old police station. The only vehicle parked there was Sheriff Barnes's squad car.

Belle sat for a moment, watching the raindrops slide down her windshield, before she sighed and turned off the engine. She glanced over at the diner, which was closed—one of the few days in the year that it wasn't open. Pulling the hood of her raincoat over her head, Belle hopped out of the car and hurried up the steps to the station.

"Hey, Sheriff," she said, as she pushed open the door.

Sheriff Barnes was seated behind his desk, looking through some papers. He glanced up at her and motioned for her to sit down in the wooden chair opposite him.

"Hi Belle," he said, nodding at her. "Thank you for coming in. The forensics team has completed processing the scene. I'm waiting for them to make a few phone calls, and then they'll be out of there."

"Oh, okay," said Belle, wondering if she should take her coat off. But the sheriff looked so serious that she decided to leave it on. "Is there anything that I can do to help?"

"Well, we've also got the medical examiner's report back," he said, peering at her over his reading glasses. "The coroner is still waiting for the toxicology report, but his preliminary findings are that Reginald was poisoned."

Belle gasped, placing her hand over her mouth. "Poisoned? Oh, my goodness!"

"Yeah, I know." He nodded. "It's not pleasant news. So, the question is, how was he poisoned?"

Belle gave him a blank look. "I don't know, Sheriff."

"Well, we're still investigating that," he said. "Our forensics team is trying to track down everything Reginald ate or drank prior to his death. But it's going to take some time. You were a server at the party. Did you see what he ate or drank?"

Belle shook her head. "Well, he refused all of the appetizers. And in the brief time that he was at my serving table, I didn't see him eat anything. But he drank some champagne."

"Right," said Sheriff Barnes, tapping his fingers on the desk. "And he wasn't sick at the party or anything?"

Belle thought back to the night before. She could picture Reginald with his debonaire smile. "He looked perfectly healthy to me. He didn't seem sick at all. But then again, I only talked to him for a little while, just before midnight."

"He died just after midnight last night," said the sheriff. "We should have more details later today."

Belle took a deep breath, thinking about the dance and the kiss that she had shared with Reginald at midnight. "I... I have no idea what he would have had before he came to the party. But in the half hour before midnight, he was only drinking champagne. He refused all the hors d'oeuvres and only drank one glass of champagne. I know, because I poured it for him."

"Well, that's a start," said the sheriff, referring to a note in his notebook. "We'll have to go through all the food and drinks at the party. I understand several witnesses saw you in the man's company around midnight."

Belle's stomach twisted, as she thought about the party. She could only imagine how put out Mr. Buchen would be about all of this. He had been so careful to make everything run smoothly at the party.

"Was it food poisoning? Are any of the other guests at risk?" she asked. There had been a massive amount of food and drink passed around—all of it gone now. There was no way of knowing what had made Reginald sick enough that it had killed him. "Has anyone else felt sick?"

"Not that I know of. But I'm having our medical team interview everyone who attended the party," said the sheriff. "The coroner will tell us what kind of poison was used. We know that it was a quick-acting poison. So far, it seems like Reginald was the only victim of it."

Belle shivered. "How could he be the only one who was poisoned?" she asked.

Sheriff Barnes had the same thought. He cleared his throat and gazed out the window. "I've interviewed some of the other guests and workers, and they said they saw you were the only one serving him drinks just before he died. And that you were, uh, seen kissing the man."

Belle's cheeks flushed red. She was glad that the sheriff wasn't looking at her—he would have seen her blush. "Yes... but I only met the guy last night! "She opened her eyes wide. "I had absolutely no reason to poison him."

The sheriff gave her an unreadable look. "I guess you wouldn't," he said, tapping his pencil on the desk. "But I have to follow up on all of my leads."

"You don't have to follow up on me!" protested Belle. "You know me! I wouldn't hurt a fly, let alone poison someone!"

"Right, yes of course, I know you," said the Sheriff, a small smile on his lips.

"I had no idea why he was flirting with me. And to be honest, I drank a glass of that champagne too." She gave the sheriff a sheepish grin. "We weren't supposed to. I'm not usually much of a drinker, but I guess I got carried away at the party."

"You also drank some of the champagne that you were serving?" asked Sheriff Barnes, suddenly interested. "From the same bottle?"

Belle nodded. "Yes, does that make a difference?"

"I'm not sure," said the policeman, his eyes narrowing as he made another note in his notebook. "That's an interesting piece of information." He glanced up. "I have to be honest with you, Belle. You're under suspicion until I can rule you out."

Belle's mouth opened in surprise. "You've got to be kidding me!"

Her surprise made the sheriff smile politely. "I'm afraid not," he said, standing up and moving toward the door of his office. "For now, I'd appreciate it if you stayed in town, in case I need to ask you any more questions."

Belle nodded. "I guess I can do that," she said. Belle understood why the sheriff thought she might be a suspect, but she guessed it was standard procedure. "It's not like I was planning on going anywhere anyway."

The man shrugged. "We have a lot of work ahead of us before we can find out what happened."

"You'll figure it out," she said, more to reassure herself than anything else. "Surely, someone with that much money had enemies. Maybe you should focus on that."

"Yes, we're working on it," said Sheriff Barnes, and he gave her a serious look. "Don't leave town, though."

Belle nodded and took a deep breath. "Of course," said Belle. "I'll let you know if I remember anything else." She paused. "Could I ask you a favor?"

"Certainly," he said, putting away his notebook. "What can I do?"

She coughed. "Well, I saw Wilma at the party last night. I hoped she didn't see me dancing with Reginald last night. You know how she can be ..."

"Ah yes, Wilma," said the sheriff. "She's one of my witnesses too." He looked at Belle with a twinkle in his eye. "Don't worry. I'll ask her not to gossip about your evening with Reginald."

"Oh good," sighed Belle, feeling relieved. "That would be a great help."

She could only imagine what Wilma may get up to if she got wind of the fact that Belle had been kissing a strange man that she had only just met at a party. Wilma would assume that she was throwing herself at men, because she needed a date. That woman was famous for trying to act as a matchmaking service in town. So far, with no success for anyone involved.

"No problem," said Sheriff Barnes. "Incidentally, how is Mr. Buchen doing? I heard that he got quite a scare last night."

"He was quite shocked," Belle replied. "You know what he's like. Very proper and all business."

"I suppose so," said the sheriff. "Well, I'll let you rest up after a late night. I'm sure that you need it."

Belle nodded and left the police station as quickly as she could. But as soon as she was out on the street, she stopped in her tracks. She realized that she had forgotten to tell the Sheriff about her co-worker, Madison, and her strange behavior the night before. She had thought Madison was her friend, but after she had accused Belle of flirting with everyone, Madison was clearly angry with her about something.

Belle sighed. She probably needed to talk to Madison and find out what was wrong, but she really didn't feel up to it now.

Whatever had gotten into Madison would just have to wait until tomorrow.

Belle drove back to the cottage looking forward to a cozy afternoon catching up on sleep, curled up on the couch next to the fire.

Chapter 9

No sooner had Belle made plans to read a book and snooze on the couch by the fire, than they were thwarted by the last person that she wanted to see.

"Belle! There you are!" Wilma Figg sang out from the living room, as soon as Belle had opened the front door. She was warming her hands by the hearth next to the Christmas tree, while Grace sat in her recliner.

Belle suppressed a groan.

Grace gave her an apologetic shrug, as Belle stepped into the house and closed the front door against the cold. "I tried to convince Wilma that you were busy, but she said it was very important," she said, meaningfully.

Belle shot her grandmother an undecipherable look before turning back to face the other woman. "What can I do for you, Wilma?"

"It's what I can do for you, my dear," Wilma smiled smugly, as she made herself comfortable on the sofa by the paper-laden coffee table. "I spoke with our Sheriff Barnes this morning and told him everything that I witnessed last night. I'm quite an important eyewitness, you see."

Belle froze. "What did you witness exactly?"

"Oh, I don't like to repeat myself. Sheriff Barnes will need to ask you all the same questions, what with the killer still being at large."

Grace's jaw dropped. "You told Sheriff Barnes that you saw the killer?"

"No, not really," said Wilma, clarifying. "But I saw a shadow that could have been a person. Possibly wearing a black dress. I definitely saw something last night."

"That could have been anybody." Belle said, skeptically. "Did you see anything at all?"

"Well, no. But I heard that perhaps it was something that the poor man ate. So, I gave the sheriff a list of all the people there that night and what they were eating, as well as all the canapes that I thought tasted revolting. I notice these things, you see. Things that other people wouldn't." She had pulled out a little notebook, in which Belle could see a bunch of notes in Wilma's tiny, cramped handwriting. "Like Mrs. Blatherwick's choice of tarts. They were kale and onion, as I recall. Terrible choice of a tart for a party."

"That was very helpful," Belle said, through gritted teeth. "I'm sure."

Mrs. Blatherwick was the head chef at the winery and had previously worked at a four-star Michelin restaurant.

Wilma looked pleased with herself. "I thought so too. It's all written in this little notebook here." She prodded her notebook like it was some sort of holy tablet that held the secrets to the mystery that had unfolded at the Buchen Winery. "We all need to help Mr. Buchen avoid any bad press. His winery, and the tourism that it brings, is very important to Cherryville. I, for one, am ready to stand by the citizens of this town."

"Very impressive," said Grace flatly. "But I really need to get on with cooking dinner—"

"So, anyway," Wilma said, looking down at her notes and ignoring Grace completely. "My nephew is here for the holidays, and I wondered if you would like to come over and meet him?"

Belle looked at Grace for assistance, but the older woman only shrugged helplessly. She tried to ignore the sinking pit that had appeared in her stomach. "Oh... Thank you, but I'm not really interested."

"Not interested?" Wilma looked aghast. "What a strange thing to say about a relative of mine! Of course you're interested." Her eyes narrowed, as she pinned Belle down with a penetrating gaze. "You were flirting with the fellow who died. I saw you kiss him! That can only mean one thing."

"I... it wasn't... I don't..."

"Yes, yes, you need a date! Of course, you do. Young woman, such as yourself."

"I really don't think—" Belle tried again, but was cut off.

Wilma stood up. "Nonsense! I'll go and call my nephew and get him to call you to set up a coffee date or something. How about tomorrow?"

Belle's face was growing redder by the second. "I would rather not."

"Of course, you would!" Wilma was already making her way toward the front door. She stopped at the entrance, turned around, and issued a last command, "It'll be lovely! Young people need a bit of a nudge now and then, don't they?"

Belle couldn't think of an answer fast enough. The door slammed shut and the two women were left alone in Grace's living room.

"So..." said Belle, taking a deep breath to steady her voice, "I guess you know who she was talking about?"

Grace nodded silently. She took off her glasses and cleaned them with the bottom of her shirt. "There's no stopping her when she gets a bee in her bonnet, I'm afraid. You don't need to show up, of course. I'm happy to have a medical emergency, if you like."

"No, no. That won't be necessary," said Belle quickly.

Grace responded with a wry smile, "Yes, I thought so. You're probably the only young person in town who Wilma hasn't tried to set up on a date." She put her glasses back on and regarded Belle behind their lenses with an amused expression before continuing, "So... you had a good time at that party and made some memories?" she chuckled. "That's my girl."

Belle pulled a face. "I did, actually. It was a lot of fun. Right up until we found his dead body."

"Oh, yes. Dearie me," said Gram, shaking her head. "Too bad about that fellow. But from what I've read in the magazines, he was a bit of a ladies' man. But still... It's a shame to lose a good young man like that."

"A shame indeed!" Belle agreed, without really thinking about what her grandmother was saying. Her worries about the death of Reginald Hartford had been supplanted by thoughts of having to go on a blind date with Wilma's nephew.

"You never know, you may even have fun," suggested Grace, picking up her knitting. "Now, what did Sheriff Barnes want to know?"

Belle took a deep breath and told her grandmother about what had happened at the station.

"Well, that explains it," said Grace when Belle was finished. "Poisoned! By the champagne! And the sheriff isn't ruling you out as a suspect. What a ninny."

Belle smiled tiredly. "I know. It all just seems so... odd."

"Yes, I suppose it does," said Grace. She returned to knitting and watching the snow fall outside her window.

"I mean, I was standing at my wine serving counter all evening, except for when I danced with Reginald. No one had an opportunity to put poison in the wine that I was serving. And then, I had just opened a fresh bottle of champagne for his drink, so no one could have put anything in it. I drank from that bottle too. So, I don't see how he could have been poisoned by my wine."

"Yes, I see... And the only time you were away from your counter was when you danced with Reginald?"

Belle nodded. "Yes. I nearly left my counter to help another girl out. She left her counter earlier. But I stayed put."

"Hmm," agreed Grace. "I don't suppose you can think of anyone with a motive to kill Reginald? Someone who was acting strangely at the party?"

Belle thought for a moment. "The only person who acted strangely was Madison."

Grace raised an eyebrow. "Really?" she asked. "Who is she?"

Belle shrugged. "The one who left her wine station. I don't really know her very well. She was one of the wine servers at the party. She helped me learn about the wines and was super helpful right until the night of the party. After we found Reginald, she acted like she didn't like me, or Reginald."

"How strange," said Grace, interested. "Do you think she could be the poisoner?"

Belle shook her head. "I don't know. I mean, it's possible... But what about all those people at the party? This wine tasting was a very exclusive event. Every important person in the county was there that night. Reginald was a billionaire. He could have had enemies at the party."

Grace stroked Mittens, who was making himself comfortable on her knitting. "I hope you told Sheriff Barnes all of this."

Belle sighed. "I forgot. He seemed to be more interested in asking me about the wine that I served that poor man. I think that I convinced him that I had no reason to kill Reginald. I mean, I had only just met the guy, for heaven's sake."

"Well, that's good at least," said her Gram. "You should remember to tell the sheriff about Madison the next time you see him."

Belle nodded. "Okay." She glanced back out the window, as flurries of snow swirling against the windowpane.

Grace thought for a moment. "At least you haven't been accused of murder—yet. But I think it would probably be best if you try to find out who killed Reginald all the same. I don't like the idea of anyone suspecting you. And I'm not just saying that because you're my granddaughter. They have to focus on finding the real killer. If that ninny, Sheriff Barnes, doesn't take you off the suspects list, I will go down to the station and give him a piece of my mind until he does."

Belle smiled and reached over to give Grace a hug. "Thanks, Gram. I doubt it will come to that. It's probably standard procedure. I'll go back to the winery tomorrow and talk to Madison, and maybe try to find out more about Reginald. Many of the staff from the winery have left, but there are still some there who work in the wine rooms year-round."

"Good," said Grace, nodding with approval. "You've had a crazy Christmas season this year, after helping solve the murder of that poor woman a few weeks ago. But you'll have to do it again. And don't forget, you need to arrange your date with that young relative of Wilma's tomorrow, too."

Belle shuddered. "I don't know, Gram. I'm not interested in going on a blind date with someone related to Wilma."

"Nonsense, dear. It's the only way to get her to stop trying to set you up with him. I'm sure you'll have fun. And if you don't like him, you don't have to see him again," said Grace firmly, and then turned to look out the window again, as she saw a familiar-looking truck pull up close to the house.

"Ah! Just in time, too! Looks like the delivery van has arrived with our groceries! Now, what would you like for dinner?"

Chapter 10

The next day, Belle was up early. It was a workday at the winery, and she hurried to get ready. She reversed the car out of the driveway and made her way out of town. The morning was clear, but cold. It had not snowed overnight, and the roads were dry.

As she headed out of town, the houses on either side of the road disappeared and soon gave way to tall trees and farmland.

The road leading up to the Buchen Winery was freshly cleared of snow. It looked different in the bright light of morning. The winter vineyards stretched out in regimented rows on either side of the road, waiting for spring to come and warm the soil, so that they could sprout new leaves again.

The winery was on top of a hill that had been terraced with low walls. Rosebushes, cut back for the winter, lined the sides of the driveway leading up to the house. Belle drove up and around the side of the main building, to the back. At last, she reached the parking lot where there were only five other cars parked, besides hers. The wine tasting rooms were not yet open, of course, as they only opened just before lunch. The kitchen staff would be starting on the lunch menu for the tourists, who were touring the wine region near Cherryville.

She stepped out of the car and headed inside via the staff entrance. Slipping into the kitchen, Belle walked past the large stainless-steel ovens and stoves. She spotted the server with the buzz-cut from the night before, unloading a dishwasher. Tyler. He looked surprised to see her.

"Are you working today? I thought that you were one of the casual staff who only worked here for the New Year's Eve party."

She smiled at him. "No, I'm working through January. What a way to start a new job! Can you believe it?" She nodded toward the restroom where Reginald Hartford had been found. "Do you have a minute to chat about what happened? You know, the other night."

Tyler looked around. "Okay, it's a while before our shift starts. I guess we can talk in the other room. But not for too long." He motioned her to follow him back into the tasting room. "We're expecting a delivery of wine from the cellars anytime now, so I need to stay here."

Belle agreed and followed Tyler into the other room, where they had learned about all the wines that they served at the party the other day. Clean glasses were stacked on the shelves, glinting in the morning sun. The polished oaken floorboards shone in the sunlight streaming in through the large window that stretched the length of the room. Heavy green curtains were tied back with thick cords, framing the view of the winter gardens outside.

Belle sat down on a chair at a table in the middle of the room. Tyler followed suit, but said nothing for a while. He seemed to be preoccupied by something else.

Finally, he looked up and said, "It was really weird what happened to that guy last night. That was one crazy night!" he said, shaking his head. "I think nothing like that has ever happened before here."

"Yes," agreed Belle. "Trust me, it isn't fun finding a dead body. It happened to me only the other week. I can't believe it's happening again."

Tyler looked surprised. "You found a body too?"

"Don't worry about it. That's a whole other story." Belle waved away his question. "Have you heard anything about how the guy died?"

"They said that it was a heart attack. That's what one guest said." Tyler glanced at her. "He seemed quite young to have had a heart attack, though."

Belle shook her head. "I need your help with finding out how he died. Have you ever seen him arguing with anyone? Anyone here at all?"

Tyler thought about that for a moment. "Not that I can think of. The guy was a bit of a flirt. He would chat up all the girls."

She blushed, thinking that she had been one of those girls.

"Think harder," Belle urged him. "This is important!"

"Okay, okay, I'm thinking! Jeez, why are you so uptight?" Tyler complained. He rested his elbows on the table and leaned forward in concentration. "He was mostly hanging out and talking with Madison, from what I remember."

"Madison?" Belle asked curiously. "Madison with the auburn hair?"

"That's right. I don't know how well they knew each other, but they hung out a bit and talked and laughed together. In fact, they were whispering together last night. I saw her leave the room with him," Tyler looked at Belle as if to say, "so there you go".

Belle nodded thoughtfully, remembering Madison leaving the marquee with a man in a tuxedo. From the back, she couldn't see who it was, but it could have been Reginald Hartford. And then there was the anger that Madison had suddenly directed her way after the party.

"Madison was acting a bit strangely at midnight on New Year's Eve. She seemed quite angry. Do you know what she was talking about with Reginald?"

Tyler shook his head. "Sorry, no idea. I was at my wine station, but I heard them laughing when they walked past."

"And when was this?" Belle asked him hopefully.

"Well, let me think," Tyler paused. "It must have been a few hours after the party had started. So maybe around ten in the evening?"

That was about the time that Madison left her counter and disappeared for a while.

"Okay, thanks, Tyler," Belle said as she stood. "If you think of anything else, tell me."

"Will do." He stood. "I hope that they figure out what happened."

"The police aren't telling anyone much," Belle explained. "But I really appreciate your help."

"No problem." Tyler shrugged. "It was more interesting than counting bottles of wine."

"I know, right?" Belle smiled ruefully. "But hey, we should probably get ready for our shift."

Belle wasn't sure that Tyler had given her much information. It seemed like he had just confirmed that Madison knew the victim, which Belle already suspected. But why would she be angry? And why were they whispering together?

She racked her brains for any memory of Madison from last night. She was hiding something, Belle was sure about it. But what was it? Something was nagging at the back of Belle's mind, but it wasn't coming to her. She decided the best thing to do would be to find Madison and ask her if they could have a chat.

Suddenly, her phone beeped. It was a text from an unknown number.

Hi. Wilma gave me your number. This is Edward Figg. Would you like to go out for a drink this evening?

"Great," she muttered to herself, "This is exactly what I need right now."

She was about to text him back when her phone beeped again.

We could meet at the diner in town.

Belle exhaled with annoyance, but she paused and breathed in deeply before typing back a polite answer. Gram had said that it was the only way to get Wilma to stop trying to set her up with this particular relative and she was probably right. She may as well get it over with. Like pulling a Band-Aid off.

Belle would be finished with work by 5 p.m. and that would give her enough time to drive back into town. She texted a message back.

Sure, how about around 6 p.m.?

He replied quickly.

Sounds great. See you then.

Belle stared at her phone. She was about to tell him that she'd changed her mind and text that something came up when the phone beeped again.

Have you figuration out who did in the billionaire yet?

It was full of typos. The name showed above the message. Grace Beaumont.

Belle's grandmother was still learning how to use predictive text.

Belle chuckled and texted back.

I'm working now.

Gram's message came back.

Good luck, grill! I mean, girlie. And if anyone can solvate it, it's you! You're the smartest person I know.

Belle smiled at all the typos on her phone.

Suddenly, a voice spoke behind her. "Belle! You're back."

Belle spun around to see Madison standing behind her with a knowing look on her face. "We should talk, don't you think?"

Chapter 11

Madison strutted off into the garden, as Belle followed her into the cold winter air, marveling at how Madison could walk around in such high heels. She wore a stylish, long, gray dress, whereas Belle was wearing dark jeans and her Doc Martens.

As Belle caught up with her, Madison whirled around and put her hands on her hips. "Belle, I thought that you were my friend." She looked angry.

Belle was at a loss. "I am your friend," she replied, confused. As much as a person could be a friend to someone that they had just met.

"Then, how could you do that to me?" Madison asked, her eyes wet with unshed tears.

"Um—" Belle looked about for help. "Do what?" Belle wracked her brain to figure out what Madison was talking about.

"Dance with Reginald, of course! I saw you kiss him at midnight, you know. Don't think that I didn't," Madison said, her tone bitter. "That should have been me."

The penny dropped in Belle's brain with a bit of a clang. She remembered now. Madison had mentioned just before the party that she was going to spend New Year's Eve with someone special.

Her someone special had been Reginald Hartford.

"I'm sorry. I really didn't know that you two were together," Belle said cautiously, pulling her coat around her against the crisp morning air. "I had no idea."

"We were supposed to leave the party together after I finished work. He was going to take me home with him and then we were going to spend New Year's Day together as well. But he told me at the party that he thought we should take a break." Madison said, staring at Belle with accusing eyes. "I didn't take him seriously, of course."

"Oh," Belle said, not knowing what else to say. "I'm sorry."

"Oh?" Madison repeated, her tone dripping with ice. "Is that all you have to say? You stole my man and then acted like he was yours the whole night. I saw the way that you were looking at him."

Belle opened her mouth to object, but shut it again. She had merely thought that he was a handsome man showing her some attention, so she had enjoyed a dance. And after the glass of champagne, she had just been having fun at a party, nothing more. She couldn't have been dancing with him for longer than twenty minutes before he disappeared, after the turn of midnight.

"I'm sorry. I really didn't know—"

"It doesn't matter if you knew or not. You should have kept your hands to yourself," Madison snapped. "And as for kissing him—"

"I didn't really touch him, and I didn't kiss him," Belle said in a small voice. "He kissed me." Too late, she realized it was absolutely the wrong thing to say.

Madison sneered at her. "Are you telling me he didn't fancy me anymore, that he fancied you instead? Whatever. I'm sure it was enough to make me look like a fool in front of everyone."

Belle was at a loss for what to say. "I—" she stammered. "I didn't mean—"

"Well, at least you're not denying it," Madison said, her eyes like daggers in Belle's direction. "I heard you asking Tyler questions about Reginald."

"I thought that I would ask around to see if anyone saw anything suspicious during the evening. You know, like someone tampering with the drinks, or poisoning something," Belle said, desperately trying to change the subject.

"And you think that I'm a suspect?" Madison replied, her eyes widening in surprise and then narrowing again into dark green slits.

"Not at all," Belle backpedaled, although Madison certainly looked like she was ready to kill someone. "I was just trying to help Sheriff Barnes figure out what happened to Reginald."

"Well, I think that you should leave it to the police," Madison said with a sneer. "I've got nothing to do with him dying. But if you want my theory on how he died, then here it is."

Belle stared back at her with a frown. "And what is that?"

"I think Reginald killed himself. He was a self-absorbed guy, but he knew that I would move on pretty quickly if he broke up with me, so no doubt he decided that it would be better to take his own life than face me," Madison replied. She put her hand on her hip in a defiant gesture.

Belle stared at Madison in disbelief. "You really think that he did that?" It struck her that the other woman seemed a little self-absorbed herself.

"Yeah, that's what I think." A small smirk played around Madison's mouth.

"That's a horrible thing to say," Belle replied, shaking her head.

"It might be the truth, though," Madison said with a small shrug of her shoulders. "So, you can take it or leave it."

"But if you could just let me know what wines you saw him drink." Belle tried to sound as reasonable as she could.

"I didn't see him drink anything, except champagne," Madison answered. "And weren't you the one supplying him with that? That's what I told the police, anyway." She tossed her long, thick auburn hair over her shoulder again, and Belle couldn't help wondering how she got her hair so shiny and soft looking. Then the words of what the other woman had said sank in.

"What did you tell the police?" Belle asked, her eyes widening.

"That you were the only one supplying him with drinks all evening, and that if he drank anything that made him ill, you would be the only one who would have given it to him."

Belle's face blanched at this statement. "But that's not true at all."

"Well, you shouldn't have spent so long on the dance floor with him, dancing cheek to cheek if you didn't want people to think that it was more than just work-related," Madison said, her tone full of resentment. "You both deserve exactly what you get."

"You can't mean that. No one deserves to die, I'm sure." Belle was shocked.

"Some people do. And some people should be quizzed by the police," Madison said, her tone full of steel.

"I think we should get back to work," Belle said awkwardly.

Madison waved that off dismissively. "No matter, Belle. It's not my problem." She turned on her heel and walked away with a flick of her hair over her shoulder.

Belle stared after her for a moment, feeling slightly shell-shocked. She had felt that Madison was angry with her, but until today, she had no idea what she was angry about. She had heard that some women got jealous if their boyfriends flirted with other women, but never thought that she would be on the end of this type of jealousy herself.

Belle walked back to the wine tasting room in a daze, still feeling quite shaken by Madison's reaction to her questioning and wondering whether the woman was not quite right in the head.

So far, her efforts to figure out what happened to Reginald had fallen flat. And with Madison actively telling lies to Sheriff Barnes about her possibly serving the victim poisoned wine, she was worse off than before.

Belle sighed as she polished wineglasses, ready for the tourists coming through for the day, still feeling deflated by the encounter with Madison.

All she had found out so far was that Reginald was a bit of a flirt, which she knew already. Also, that Madison was jealous of Belle dancing with him, and was quite possibly mentally unwell too.

The other woman had been so angry with her that it was several minutes before Belle remembered what Madison had said about Reginald. What exactly had she said? That he deserved what he got, or something to that effect? Could Madison have been so jealous that she had poisoned him herself? To kill him?

It was possible that Madison had served him poisoned wine sometime in the evening. Any of the servers at the New Year's Eve party could have done so. But as far as Belle knew, no one other than Madison had a motive to kill the billionaire.

Belle shook her head slightly. She couldn't say why, but somehow, she didn't think that Madison was capable of doing something like that. Then again, jilted women throughout history had been capable of many things.

Hell hath no fury like a woman scorned, indeed.

With her auburn hair, Madison had certainly appeared as nothing less than furious that morning.

Chapter 12

"And that one?" said the woman in activewear, her overpriced sunglasses propped on the top of her head. "How expensive is that one?"

She was one of the many tourists who were passing through the wine region on their way to the ski slopes, and she was pointing at a bottle of wine on the shelf behind Belle. Her companion stood next to her looking bored.

"It's about two hundred dollars a bottle," said Belle, who by now had learned a lot about the Buchen wines that had been such a mystery before, "It's a good wine, but that's not why we charge so much for it. It has a very small production. There were only a few bottles of that particular vintage produced that year."

"Okay," said the woman, "that makes perfect sense. Now, what about the bottles on special offer? How much are those?"

"Well, I don't think anything is on special offer—"

"Never mind. I'll take twelve bottles of that first one then," said the woman. "I need them for my friends back home. They will go nuts when they see this."

It never ceased to amaze Belle how much money people were willing to pay for wine. Belle rang in the order, noting down how many cases of each variety the woman wanted. "We can ship it to you if you like," said Belle, "but it might be expensive, as the freight costs will—"

"That's fine," said the woman, waving her credit card. "I don't mind paying."

"I want to see where the billionaire died," said her companion, strolling up to the counter. He had a camera on his chest that he had removed from the bag, ready for some action. "I heard that he drank some bad wine. Is that true?"

"Who told you that?" asked Belle, trying to keep her voice level.

"Oh, you know, here and there. It's all over the news. Read about it." He waved his phone at her as evidence before putting it back in his pocket. "They say he drank bad wine here."

"Oh no, babe!" exclaimed the woman. "Don't say that. I just bought twelve bottles of it. Is it bad?"

Mr. Buchen suddenly appeared, smiling at his guests. "Oh, I wouldn't believe everything you hear on the news. An unfortunate medical emergency, but one I'm sure will not be repeated." He smiled in a way that Belle noticed was not as warm as usual.

He's hiding his nerves well.

"I don't know," said the woman in the activewear. "If there is something wrong with the wine, then there's a chance that I might get sick, too. I have allergies, you know."

Mr. Buchen laughed heartily at this remark and then, lifting the most expensive bottle of wine from the shelf, poured three glasses. "Cheers!" he said, lifting one to his lips and taking a drink. "And here's to a Happy New Year."

The woman and her companion waited for Mr. Buchen to drink the wine before picking up the glasses themselves. When the owner of the winery didn't fall down dead, they drank too.

"See? It's a perfectly balanced vintage. Nothing wrong with it!" exclaimed Mr. Buchen, smiling widely at them all. "Notes of currant and blackberry. Perfect with our highly acclaimed rump steak. If you die of anything here at the Buchen Winery, it will be from overindulgence, not bad wine!"

The activewear woman applauded Mr. Buchen for his wit, and they all laughed together.

"Babe, I was right," said the woman. "This is what all the famous people drink." They moved off to continue their tour of the winery, a smiling Mr. Buchen waving them on their way.

When they had left, the smile on her boss's face faded and he suddenly looked quite tired. He glanced back at Belle. "That's how you deal with questions about the unfortunate incident at the party. Just keep saying that it was a medical emergency and that nobody drank bad wine here. Understood?"

Belle nodded.

"It's hard enough getting a business like this off the ground without negative reports like that circulating," said Mr. Buchen, rubbing his forehead. "There will be a lot of visitors coming through and we don't want them to not come here because they think that someone died from the wine. We can't afford any kind of bad press. I wish whoever did this hadn't..."

"I understand, sir," said Belle, feeling quite sorry for her boss. It couldn't be easy to have this kind of thing occur during the busiest time of the year. "Is there anything else that I can do for you, sir?"

"No, no, that's fine." Mr. Buchen glanced at the clock, then looked back at Belle. "I have to go to a meeting now. You're doing well, Belle. I may even revise your status as casual staff at the end of the month. If we need more help, I'll let you know."

Belle smiled. "Thank you, Mr. Buchen," she said. "That would be great." The job would keep her going until she found something better.

She watched as Mr. Buchen walked quickly out of the tasting room and toward his office.

"I don't know how he does that," said Tyler, arriving from the cellar with the shipment of wines for Belle to check. The guy was dressed in his usual black polo-neck and black pants, his buzzcut neatly standing on end. "Drinking all this wine every day. He must have a liver made of steel."

"He looked nervous though, didn't he?" asked Belle, glancing around to make sure Mr. Buchen was out of sight for now. "I'm sure the news of Reginald's death hasn't been great for business."

"He doesn't look happy, that's for sure," said Tyler, shaking his head and sighing. "I heard a few guests cancelled their stay here after hearing the news. But then a lot more are coming here to have a look at the place where a rich guy died. It's morbid, really, but I guess business is business."

"Yes, a billionaire's death must be both good and bad for business," said Belle, checking the shipment, then writing "Checked" on the box.

Tyler laughed uneasily. "Yeah... I suppose..."

Belle watched Tyler walk away and suddenly felt the need for caffeine. She checked her watch. It was nearly mid-afternoon, and she was due for a break. She didn't have any customers at her station right then, so she pulled off her apron and slipped down the hall, heading to the kitchen where the staff coffee machine stood.

As she walked down the hall, she passed the stairs leading to Mr. Buchen's office. Just then, the door opened and he came out, followed by another man. They were speaking in low voices, but she thought that Mr. Buchen said something about money and construction.

Belle quickly picked up the pace and passed them, heading for the kitchen. As she did so, she took a brief sideways glance at the man following Mr. Buchen. He looked vaguely familiar, not that Belle could see much of his face, but she could at least see that he was wearing a pricey-looking, yet ill-fitting, suit. There was something about that man, but she couldn't quite put her finger on it.

Then she remembered.

It was the man from the party! The one who had visited her wine station and who had later bumped into Reginald on the dance floor. Reginald had said that he was someone's older brother, but at the time, she hadn't taken him seriously. She remembered because he had been the only person at the party not looking happy to be there. She knew she had seen his face before.

What was he back here for?

She waited in the hall while the two men walked down the stairs and headed out to the foyer, curiosity getting the better of her. She remembered the man in the suit had looked at Reginald with disapproval. He looked similarly unsmiling now. He certainly wasn't as handsome as Reginald and looked more like an accountant than a playboy.

As the men stood in the foyer talking, Belle couldn't help herself and moved behind a large fake flower display, hoping to overhear their conversation.

"It's just too risky. I'm telling you," Mr. Buchen said, "We should wait until the police find the murderer and then we can start the project."

The other man snorted. "Are you mad? Who knows when that will be? It could be months. The police are already stumped and they've had plenty of time to investigate the death of my brother," replied the man in the suit. "I'm telling you, it's not safe to wait."

His brother?

Belle gasped.

He was Reginald's brother?

"It's not safe to start either!" said Mr. Buchen, with a hint of panic in his voice. "The police have interviewed everyone who was at that party. They may come back for more questioning! They're looking at the staff too. I heard them say so. I've been providing them with the information, and I'll tell them more."

The two men turned away and it was difficult for Belle to hear, but she could still catch some words.

"Don't be ridiculous! They have no evidence against any of the staff. They're doing their job, that's all," scoffed the stranger. "Anyway, I had a look at your numbers and you need this project to start within two weeks, or you're going to sink! You'll be bankrupt soon enough if it doesn't. Believe me, I know what it takes to get things done around here."

There was the sound of the front door opening, and then their voices got fainter as they moved outside. The door slammed shut and Belle jumped. It took a while for her to regain her breath and when she did, she stood for a good while chewing her lip, as she tried to make sense of what she had just heard.

What did Mr. Buchen mean when he said the project wasn't safe? And what exactly was Reginald's brother so keen to start building?

Chapter 13

Marylin's Diner was still warm with the smell of frying bacon and the chatter of locals. It wasn't the best place to meet for an evening date, but at least the menu had a great burger and chips.

Belle let the door swing shut behind her and walked up to the counter. "Hi, Marilyn," she said, "How was your Christmas?"

"Wonderful," said the buxom owner behind the counter. "The kids were off school and we got a white Christmas. Are you here for your blind date?"

"Yup," replied Belle, unsurprised that word of her date had gotten around. In fact, it would be a miracle if the entire town didn't know already.

"I'll be there in a minute to take your order," she said, as she busied herself with the coffee machine. "Your date is sitting at table eight. He looks nervous." She winked.

Belle nodded and looked around the diner. A bookish young man in a navy-blue turtleneck sweater was sitting at table eight with his back toward the counter, looking around. He already had a cup of coffee in front of him, but looked out of place in this diner with his round glasses and his hair neatly slicked back. She walked toward him and stood there for a moment, unsure of what to say.

"Hi," she said, before sitting down opposite him.

The man in navy turned around and smiled nervously. "Hi," he replied and stood up to shake her hand. "You must be Belle," he said as he stood. He was a little taller than her, but not by much. "I'm Edward," he said, "Edward Figg."

"It's nice to meet you, Edward," Belle said as she sat down. "You look a little like your Aunt Wilma."

"I take after my mother, who is her sister," he replied as he sat back down. "Do you want to order?"

Belle nodded and looked at the menu. She had eaten here so many times, she already knew what she wanted. "I'll have a mushroom burger and chips," she said decisively. "And a coffee." She looked at Edward, who was still looking at the menu. "I know you are not supposed to drink coffee at night, but it doesn't keep me awake."

Marylin suddenly appeared, with some water for the table, and then asked what they would like to eat. "My usual please, Marylin," Belle said.

"Just some soup for me," said Edward. "I'm not very hungry."

Belle looked at him for a moment. "Eat something," she suggested. "The food here is very good."

"No, really, I'm not hungry," he said as he took a sip of water, "but I do like soup."

Belle could tell already that Edward Figg was not her Prince Charming. She wasn't sure if it was his general nervousness, or that he wouldn't order much to eat while she had just ordered a big plate of food.

"Look," she said, "I'm sure Wilma forced you to meet with me, just like she talked me into it, so no pressure. Let's enjoy our coffee or soup or whatever, and then we can tell your aunt it didn't work out. No harm done."

The anxiety on the poor man's face lifted and he looked very relieved.

For a moment Belle was not sure whether or not to be offended.

"That sounds like a good idea. I'm sorry if my aunt has been too pushy. She's keen for me to find someone and settle down."

"It's all right," said Belle, entertained. "She does this to everyone in town. She's a sweet and caring woman, but she can be overbearing. And too managerial."

Edward pushed his glasses up and nodded empathically. "Tell me about it," he said between sips of coffee. He looked at Belle. "So, how long have you lived in this town?"

"All my life. Except for a short time in the city," replied Belle. She didn't enjoy talking about herself and changed the subject. "So, what do you do for a living, Edward? What's your job?"

Edward looked at her; his eyes seemed to focus on something beyond Belle. "I work in a library," he replied. "I'm the librarian at one of the bigger libraries in the city."

"Oh," said Belle, "I guess you like books then?"

"I love them," said Edward. "There's nothing better than getting lost in a book. I spend most of my free time there too. If fact, that's where I met my boyfriend..." He suddenly stopped talking, stricken by what he had just said.

"Your boyfriend?" prompted Belle, sipping her coffee, amused at the way the blind date was turning out very differently to what Wilma clearly expected.

"I... yes. Anyway, enough about me."

"Okay," said Belle. "Well, you know, if you tell your aunt that you're gay and have a boyfriend, then maybe she will stop setting you up on dates. I'm sure she will be fine with it."

"I don't know," said Edward, glancing toward the counter. "It's a small town and people can get a little weird about that sort of thing around here."

"They do, but they also accept people more than you think. Look at Wilma. She's always over-organizing everything so that it goes completely wrong. The Christmas Carol Singalong turned into a complete shemozzle, but we still had fun. We're all quite used to her now."

Edward looked a little struck. "She's not that bad, surely?"

"Want to bet?" said Belle. She grinned at him. "Everyone just lets her be who she is."

"Well, my boyfriend is rather handsome." He smiled shyly. "Perhaps she may like him. His name is Tom, and he's very well read. We've been together for over a year now."

Belle smiled. "I'm sure she will like him."

Marylin arrived with Belle's burger and coffee and Edward's soup. Belle thanked her and took a big bite of her burger. Once again, it was delicious.

She chewed for a moment and then said, "So, what does your boyfriend do?"

"He's an investment banker," he replied, sipping a spoonful of soup. "He works in the city."

Belle nodded. "That sounds like fun. But then, I don't know what an investment banker actually does." She drank some water and watched Edward for a moment.

"He deals with some very rich clients. Helps them invest in things to make money." The guy took a delicate sip of soup from his spoon. "For instance, you know that billionaire who died the other day? Reginald Hartford, I think his name was? Well, my boyfriend dealt with all his financial affairs."

Belle nearly choked on her coffee. "What, really? I mean, that's interesting," she said.

"It is, but it's also stressful and he doesn't like to talk about work too much at home. He will be in town over the next couple of days, and I can introduce him to everyone."

"Great," said Belle, trying to think up a way of directing the conversation back to this Tom-the-investment-banker's work. "So, I guess he would have some idea about Reginald's business affairs? Would he know if anyone would have wanted to kill Reginald?"

"I'm not sure," replied Edward, "He might. Why do you ask?"

Belle paused and then decided it was best to tell him if he was to be any help. She looked around the diner and then lowered her voice. "I was working at the winery where Reginald Hartford died the other night. The police think someone killed him by serving him poisoned wine at the New Year's Eve party."

"Heavens!" Edward showed her a shocked face. "But why?" He leaned in, suddenly intrigued. Her date was becoming chattier by the minute now that he didn't feel like he was on a date anymore. "Was it for his money? Surely, no one would kill someone just because they pretended to be rich."

"Pretended? Are you saying Reginald wasn't rich at all?" asked Belle.

"Oh, yes. He was very rich once, but he had to sell part of his business twenty years ago because the company ran into financial difficulties." Edward paused for a minute, thinking. "It didn't help that Reginald had several poor business deals, which cost him a lot of money. He was more or less bankrupt."

"Really?" said Belle, genuinely surprised, "But he seemed to be doing all right from what I remember from the papers. I saw that he owned quite a few properties at one point."

"Yes, but most of them are mortgaged to the hilt. It's how he was able to maintain his lifestyle all these years. He told people about it, too." Edward raised his eyebrows. "I know because my boyfriend worked with him not so long ago when Reginald was desperately trying to make money. It was almost sad to see how much he wanted it."

"Would Tom know anyone who wanted Reginald dead?" asked Belle, remembering the man in the ill-fitting suit who had come to the winery the other day to talk about a secret construction project with Mr. Buchen.

Edward shrugged. "I haven't really talked about this with Tom. He doesn't like to talk about his work. That's all he told me."

Belle continued to eat her meal, while she mulled over this information. She had imagined that Reginald was very rich; certainly, she had never imagined that he was bankrupt. If this was the case, then it opened a new line of enquiry for the police to follow.

"And what about his brother?" asked Belle, remembering the serious man in the suit. "He seems different. Very serious."

"Corbin Hartford?" said Edward. "I know nothing about him, only that he's a powerful man. Owns a lot of construction companies. Why do you ask?"

Belle shook her head. "No reason." She didn't want to tell Edward that she had overheard a business conversation between Corbin Hartford and Mr. Buchen. No yet anyway. Not until she had figured out what it was about.

Belle finished her dinner and thanked Edward. She said that she had to get going but asked him to come over for tea whenever he liked, and to bring Tom along too. "My Gram bakes the best apple pies. And she would love to have more people to bake for."

"Thank you, I'll come by sometime," replied Edward. "Nice meeting you. And thank you so much for your encouragement. I may even introduce my boyfriend to my Aunt Wilma."

Belle smiled widely. Her blind date hadn't turned out so badly after all!

And she was very interested in what Edward had said about Reginald's business affairs.

Chapter 14

It was mid-January already and Belle couldn't believe how much she had learned about wine in the two weeks that she had been working at the Buchen Winery. Previously, all the names of the various wines had sounded quite foreign to her: Shiraz, Merlot, Riesling, Chardonnay... But it all made more sense now. More so, because she had also learned about the various grapes used to make them.

Her work had been made even more fun because her co-workers were quite an entertaining bunch. They often joked around and chatted amongst themselves. Belle was surprised at how much they knew about the winery. They seemed to know a lot about the wine-making process. As she found out, some of them were studying wine-making and were quite knowledgeable about plants, soil, and wind, not to mention the lives and affairs of the many rich tourists that passed through on their annual holidays.

And there were many eccentric rich tourists to talk about!

There was old Mrs. Baker and her sister who hired a chauffeur to drive them through the wine regions every winter, just to buy up choice selections for their cellar. She always arrived with two yappy chihuahuas in her car. Then there was a young online influencer couple who drove a Maserati. They were always driving around, visiting tourist spots out of town so that they could pose for pictures in scenic places. And then there were the serious wine collectors who came to purchase wines for future auctions, or as investments. The visitors to the Buchen Winery were as diverse as you could imagine. But they all had one thing in common: money.

During their morning coffee breaks, all of the waiters and waitresses gathered out by the staff entrance to chat and joke about the visitors of the day. It had become a game with them to guess how people had made their money and everyone joined in.

Everyone except Madison, of course.

In fact, Madison had been avoiding all of them, including Belle, for days. It had been two weeks since Reginald's death at the New Year's Eve party, and Belle had only seen Madison a handful of times. She kept to herself. She didn't seem to want to join in on the many conversations about the billionaire that the employees whispered amongst themselves.

"Did you hear that Reginald Hartford wasn't really rich?" said Tyler, as a few of the servers stood in the morning sun sipping their coffee on their break.

It was a slow day and so far, only a couple of foreign businessmen had passed through the tasting rooms.

"No way!" said a server called Tanya. "What do you mean?"

"Well, apparently he was only pretending to be rich," said Tyler.

"Then how did he afford a brand-new Porsche?" said Tanya. "That's an expensive car. Plus, I heard that he owned his own plane."

"Belle," said Tyler, turning to her. "Did you know Reginald wasn't really rich?"

"I didn't know him that well," said Belle, carefully.

It didn't surprise her that the information Edward had mentioned the other day was now doing the rounds. If Edward had mentioned it to his Aunt Wilma, then it would be all over town like a wildfire. She hadn't mentioned it to anyone. Belle didn't want to add to any gossip until she was sure she knew whether it was true or not.

"I heard that he lost his money on some crazy property deal," said Tyler. "And that's why he was pretending to be rich."

"That makes no sense," said Tanya. "He seemed pretty rich to me. Expensive clothes, expensive cars, and he was always in the magazines with celebrities."

"I dunno," said Tyler. "Someone told me it was all lies, and that he had lost hundreds of thousands on a property development. Maybe he was never rich and was just fooling all of us."

"What do you mean he was never rich?" said a voice outside the group.

Belle turned to see Madison standing at the staff entrance. She came toward them, brushing some dust off her slacks, as she sat down on the bench with Belle.

Tyler looked uncomfortable, but nodded. "I was just saying that I heard he wasn't as rich as he pretended to be."

"But he must have been rich at some point," said Tanya, not giving up on her opinion. "Otherwise, how would he have been able to afford a Porsche? Or his own plane?"

"I don't know," said Tyler, scuffing his heel on the paving. "I heard that he lost it all."

There was a silence as everyone looked at Madison, who sat still, staring out into the vineyards. It was obvious that she was shocked which meant she had not known this news about Reginald. For a moment, Belle thought that she might have been upset.

"Well," she said in a very loud voice, so everyone could hear her. "I think that we should all get back to work."

Belle looked around and saw that several of the other servers were watching Madison as she walked back into the kitchen.

"She has been acting really strange," said Tanya in a low voice. "Ever since the New Year's Eve party when that billionaire died. I think that she was dating him."

Belle kept her thoughts to herself. She had told no one about the conversation that she had with Madison on New Year's Day, where the auburn-haired woman had shown how jealous she was of Belle for dancing with Reginald when the clock struck midnight. Not only was Belle a little embarrassed about the whole thing, but she didn't want to give Madison any more reason to be angry at her for spreading rumors about her dating a customer.

"I figured!" said Tyler, looking over his shoulder. "Dating Reginald Hartford? You don't think that she had anything to do with him dying?"

Belle quickly looked over at the kitchen entrance, but Madison had disappeared.

"I don't know," said Tanya. "She's always so mean to everyone, anyway; I wouldn't be surprised if she had something to do with it."

"She helped me learn about the wines when I first started working here," said Belle charitably. "I think she is just upset by everything that happened, like we all are."

"Yeah, right!" scoffed Tanya, rolling her eyes.

The servers continued to chat and gossip about the unsolved death of Reginald Hartford before moving on to other topics, like the latest movies coming out. Belle only half-listened because she kept thinking about Madison. She couldn't help but feel sorry for the girl. It was obvious that she was upset about what she had heard.

Excusing herself, Belle went back into the tasting room and found Madison restocking the wine glasses. "Hey Madison," she said in a friendly tone.

"Hi," said the auburn-haired woman in an icy voice.

Belle kept her voice light and easygoing as she answered, "I wanted to see if you were okay after hearing what Tyler said."

Madison looked up, and there was nothing but irritation in her eyes. "What do you care?" she said sharply.

Belle paused for a moment, trying to ignore the venom in her tone. "I care," said Belle, simply.

"Well, I don't need your pity," Madison said angrily. "I should have known that you would be happy to gossip about me behind my back!"

Belle shook her head. "Of course, I wouldn't," she said. "I didn't tell anyone about our conversation. You know, the conversation that we had two weeks ago."

Madison looked a little relieved, and surprised. "I'm sure everyone already knows I was dating him," she said in a low voice. "But I don't want them to know he had promised me everything. I don't want them to know that he had even hinted at an engagement ring."

"I haven't told anyone," said Belle firmly.

"I feel like a complete fool!" exclaimed Madison suddenly. "I thought that he loved me! He promised me everything, and I actually believed him." She wiped away an angry tear. "But of course, I should have known. I'm only a waitress and he was a rich guy with property deals. But now I hear he was only pretending to be rich and treating us all like fools..."

Belle could almost feel the waves of fury coming off Madison.

"I'm really sorry," she said sympathetically. "I wish there was something I could do."

"I just want to forget about him," said Madison with a bitter laugh. "Just pretend the whole thing never happened!" She took several deep breaths and tried to calm down. "You did nothing wrong, actually," said Madison in a hard voice. "And I shouldn't take it out on you. He fooled you, just like me."

Belle's memory of the brief dance and kiss at midnight was already blurry and fading. Compared to Madison's dreams of marrying Reginald, Belle thought she had hardly been fooled by Reginald on quite the same scale as the other woman.

"You know what the funny thing is? I wouldn't have cared that he had no money, as long as he was honest with me." She looked away, her shoulders tense. "I need to get back to work."

Belle watched as Madison polished the dusty wine bottles that had been brought up from the cellar and decided she had done all she could.

The woman was obviously furious, and there was nothing Belle could do to help.

But could she have been furious enough to have killed Reginald?

Chapter 15

Belle had returned from the tasting room to re-join the others in the back when Mr. Buchen appeared. He looked a little flustered and annoyed. "Does anyone know where Madison is?" he said.

Tyler looked around. "She was here a minute ago—"

"She's in the tasting room," interrupted Belle. "She may need a minute. She just... ah... heard some bad news." Belle shot Tyler a look that told him not to say anything about what had happened, but he merely shrugged.

Mr. Buchen frowned, but he didn't push it. "I need everyone to come with me." He looked at Belle sternly. "Everyone who's back here should be in the staff room now."

The staff room was down the hall and to the left, overlooking the small parking lot at the back. It was a long room, with a few chairs and a couple of doors leading to the staff restrooms. A row of ten lockers stretched along the wall under the windows. Since there were fewer lockers than staff at the winery and only a few people were assigned a locker. That hadn't worried Belle, particularly as she had kept her bag in her car every day. She had only come back here to use the restroom now and then.

As everyone moved toward the staff room, Tyler held back, turning to Belle. "What's going on?"

Belle shrugged. "I don't know. But I'm sure we'll find out soon enough."

When all the servers got to the staff room, Belle was surprised to see Sheriff Barnes standing with his arms crossed and wearing a grim expression. His deputy, Officer Derek, was standing there too with a little metal suitcase full of forensic testing equipment. The wintery light from the windows fell on the unit of lockers, and all the locker doors were ajar, as if someone had opened them with a master key.

"What's going on...?" Tyler asked, but Mr. Buchen shushed him with a wave of his hand.

Sheriff Barnes looked at each of them. "I'm Sheriff Barnes from Cherryville. Local police have called us in to assist, because we have specialist chemical testing equipment." He waved at the metal suitcase that Officer Derek was holding. "And also, because local police are short on staff over the holiday season. I have some questions to ask." His eyes fell upon Madison, as she walked toward the group from the tasting room. She was clearly upset, and looked as if she had been crying. "If that's all right," he added, glancing quizzically at her.

Everyone nodded politely. Madison did too.

"One question," said the Sheriff. "Just a simple question and we can all be done here. Locker number three. Whose is it?" He pointed to a locker near the end of the unit. "That would be this one."

Belle looked at the other servers, who appeared to be trying to remember the numbers of their lockers, and if they had even been assigned one at all.

"Mine," said Madison, raising her hand, her voice slightly shaky. "Why do you ask?"

The Sheriff nodded and motioned for his deputy, who went to pull the locker door open. Everyone crowded around as he opened the door a little wider and pulled out a little bag of powder. It was white.

"Is that drugs?!" Belle asked, looking at the Sheriff for confirmation.

"No," he said slowly, "it's arsenic."

Belle gasped and Tyler exclaimed, "What?"

The Sheriff continued to speak, "And if you look here, underneath the locker—" he opened it again and pointed his pen below the lowest shelf— "there's a little spill." Belle's eyes followed his pen to see a thin white line. "We've already tested it, which is why we knew to look in this locker."

"Ar-arsenic?" said Madison weakly. "What? That can't be right!"

The sheriff nodded. "Arsenic. That's correct."

"But who keeps arsenic near a restaurant?" Tyler exclaimed. "That's for rat poison or something!"

The sheriff nodded again. "That would be correct." He paused and glanced around the room. "It's also the poison that killed Reginald Hartford. He drank champagne laced with arsenic at the New Year's Eve party, and it was the last thing that he ever did."

There was a shocked silence in the room. All eyes turned to Madison.

Madison shook her head in disbelief. "I don't know how that ended up in my locker. I didn't put it there." Her voice was still shaky, but grew more certain with every word she spoke.

Sheriff Barnes exchanged a long look with Officer Derek. He turned back to Madison. "You seem pretty sure of that," he observed.

"Well, yes," said Madison slowly. "Why would I put poison in my own locker? It's not like we have rats at the winery... and anyway —"

"Yes?" said Sheriff Barnes.

Madison paused, then exhaled slowly. "Anyway, if I wanted to kill someone with arsenic, I would have to be pretty stupid to hide it in my locker, for heaven's sake. Someone else must have put it there." She rolled her eyes as she said this, as if her innocence was so obvious it warranted no further discussion.

"That's a good point," said Officer Derek, nodding slightly to the sheriff.

Madison looked around at everyone else for support, but they were all staring at the sheriff and Officer Derek. "Well, what else could it be?" she demanded after a moment's silence.

"It's true, sir," said Belle. "She makes a good point."

The sheriff stared at Madison again for what felt like an uncomfortably long time. Then he looked around the room again, exhaling slowly. Turning to Officer Derek, he unclipped his handcuffs from his belt. "I'm going to have to ask you all to stand back. We need to take Madison in for questioning."

Madison gasped. "Questioning? About what? I told you, someone else must have put that in my locker!" She looked back and forth at everyone as people backed away from her.

"I'm sorry, Madison," said Officer Derek. "But if that is true, then you had better with us and answer all of our questions truthfully, so that we can clear you in no time."

"O-okay," said Madison, her voice trembling. "I... I guess." She looked around again at everyone with pleading eyes as the sheriff got the handcuffs ready. "There's no need for handcuffs. I'll come and answer all of your stupid questions. You all know that I didn't do this! You know that, right? Someone is trying to frame me!"

Everyone followed in shock as Sheriff Barnes and Officer Derek led Madison out to the waiting squad car at the front. They helped her into the back of the squad car and shut the door.

"What just happened?" said Belle faintly as they watched the car drive off down the hill at a smooth pace, followed by Officer Derek's motorcycle. "Madison couldn't have done something like that."

Tyler looked as if he wanted to say something, but his mouth remained closed tightly. He finally spoke. "I don't know about that. She seems pretty angry most of the time. And we all know that she was dating that rich guy."

"I guess, but I still don't think that it could have been her," said Belle in a voice that sounded much less certain than she meant it to. She glanced around at the other servers, but they were all staring after the receding police vehicles, looking confused and worried. Someone asked if Madison could be planning to poison any of them.

"Okay, everyone, show is over," said Mr. Buchen, clapping his hands. He looked quite relieved that the police had left his premises. "Let's get back to work. Now, where was I?" He stalked off back into the building to his office, muttering, "I hope the tourists on the cellar tour didn't see any of that."

The other staff members looked at each other for a moment, then slowly dispersed and got back to work. Only Belle and Tyler remained standing at the entrance.

Just then, a couple of expensive cars pulled into the driveway and two foreigners in business suits, cell phones glued to their ears, spilled out. They headed up to the front door, talking energetically in a European language. "Which way to the tasting room?" asked one of them in careful English, looking at Belle expectantly. "I'm here to try this year's catalogue. We're meeting Mr. Buchen. Can you tell him we're here?"

"The tasting room is this way," said Tyler, pointing toward the building. "I'll show you." He led the new customers inside, while Belle followed, deep in thought.

Was Madison capable of poisoning someone? She certainly had a temper, but did that mean she was capable of murder?

Belle felt sick thinking about it. What Madison had said really stuck with her. If she had secretly put poison into Reginald's wine at the party, then why would she hide the evidence in her own locker? It would have been—as Madison had said—quite a stupid thing to do.

But then again, Madison had thought that a billionaire playboy wanted to marry her and whisk her away. Maybe she had been so blinded by love and the thought of living an affluent lifestyle that she hadn't been thinking rationally.

She had certainly been furious with jealousy when she saw Reginald dance with me.

And then Madison had been even more upset when she had found out that Reginald was not as rich as he had appeared to be. Perhaps she had been sufficiently angry at her would-be boyfriend to kill him.

But then again, reasoned Belle to herself as she arranged glasses of wine for the businessmen, Madison only found out about Reginald's lack of wealth after he died.

Or had she?

Belle frowned as a thought occurred to her. Could Madison possibly have known Reginald was playing her for a fool? Would that have been sufficient motive to kill him?

Chapter 16

"This is one of the best red wines of the Buchen catalogue," said Tyler to the group of suits. "As you can see, we have an extensive range, with unique qualities for every type of consumer." He turned and whispered under his breath to Belle, "Can you please fetch Mr. Buchen?"

Belle jumped, startled out of her deep thoughts about Madison. "Sure," she said, glad she didn't have to partake in the sales conversation today. She hurried through the foyer and up the stairs to Mr. Buchen's office and knocked on the door.

"Come in," said a voice.

She pushed open the door, then jumped in surprise when she saw Corbin Hartford standing there instead of Mr. Buchen. He looked as neat as a pin in an outsized suit like before, his hair slicked back from his prominent forehead. Belle recalled Reginald's debonaire looks and couldn't help but compare the two and wonder how they could have been related.

"Oh! I'm sorry. I was looking for Mr. Buchen. There are some businessmen downstairs who are saying that they're here to meet him."

"You look familiar," said Corbin, frowning and looking at Belle like some puzzle that he couldn't quite put together. "Have I seen you someplace before?"

"Yes," she said, clearing her throat politely. "I served you some champagne at the New Year's Eve party. The night that... that your brother died." She swallowed, then took the opportunity as it presented itself. "I wanted to say that I'm very sorry for your loss."

"Oh, right," he said expressionlessly. "You were one of those girls dancing with him."

One of those girls?

Belle was caught off guard. Her mouth fell open at his dismissive tone.

She fortunately didn't need to think of anything to say, as just then Mr. Buchen appeared behind her in the doorway. "I'm right here, Belle. I'll go downstairs and see them." He turned to Corbin. "Ready?"

"Absolutely," said Corbin. "Let's go."

Belle stood there, staring after them as they walked down the stairs. Then she followed them to the tasting room, marveling at how calm Corbin Hartford was. There was something quite unpleasant about his demeanor, as if he didn't have a heart. Belle remembered his disapproving face that night when the man bumped into Reginald as he was celebrating the New Year on the dance floor, his champagne glass in hand.

Corbin Hartford didn't seem very upset about his brother's death.

She suddenly remembered the little plastic bag of white powder that Sheriff Barnes had pulled out of Madison's locker. She watched Corbin with suspicion, as he walked into the tasting room with Mr. Buchen for the meeting. How easy would it have been for someone to drop some of that powder into Reginald's wineglass on the dance floor? It had been so crowded that no one would have noticed. And Corbin had bumped into his brother on the dance floor, so he had certainly been standing close enough.

The businessmen had gathered in a group, talking among themselves. Mr. Buchen welcomed them to the winery and introduced Corbin. Corbin shook each of their hands looking very much a part of the business group.

"Now let's go over the business proposal, shall we?" announced Mr. Buchen. "We have quite a lot to discuss."

As they moved to the conference room, her boss fixed Belle with a commanding look. "Please serve everyone a sample of the Blanc de Blanc, the Blanc de Noir, and the Rosé," he instructed. "And don't mix them up."

Belle fetched the wine bottles that he had asked for and followed them to the conference room. She bustled about, filling crystal glasses with the wines and handing them out all while watching Corbin out of the corner of her eye.

The men sniffed and sipped their wines, making comments about the taste and how it compared to other expensive brands. They were particularly interested in profit margins. Mr. Buchen seemed excited about whatever project they were about to discuss.

Belle was still trying to figure out what was going on, but it sounded like he needed more investment money for his business.

After about thirty minutes, Mr. Buchen waved Belle and Tyler away. "That's the end of the tasting, gentlemen," he said. "Now let's get down to business. If you could all follow me into the conference room."

Belle followed the men into a business room to the side of the tasting bar. She took orders for coffee and rushed off to make them, glad that she didn't have to be in there with the businessmen talking about numbers and profits.

It took a few moments to prepare all the coffees using the modern machine in the kitchen. She carried them into the conference room on a large silver tray, walking backward into the swing door, so that she could open it without hands.

As she entered, Corbin Hartford was standing at the front of the conference room, a presentation showing on a large-screen TV on the wall, while the other businessmen sat around the heavy oak table. "This is just an overview of the project," Corbin was saying when she walked in, his arms waving around to emphasize his points. "Of course, the numbers aren't firm yet since we haven't finalized everything—"

Belle's eyes widened. Could this be the project they had been talking about the other day? She tried to set the coffee cups out as slowly as possible, as she snuck glances at the presentation. There was a map and some architectural drawings of a building. It looked like a hotel. The words "Hyatt" and "Luxury Hotel" were written over the architectural drawings in fancy lettering. Whatever it was, it looked like a big project, and it definitely involved major construction.

Her curiosity piqued, she continued to set a coffee down in front of each of the businessmen, while listening closely to what was being discussed.

Was this being built on the winery grounds?

She watched as Mr. Buchen passed around documents with more details about the project. The businessmen nodded and took notes. They looked excited about it.

"Well, this all sounds very interesting," said one man as he passed around the last document. "When will you have more details for us?"

Corbin smiled at him. "I hope that we can present a more detailed proposal to you soon, so that we can get started on this project. It's one of the biggest opportunities I've seen in a long time. And I'm interested in continuing my brother's work through my own construction company."

His construction company?

Edward had definitely told her that Reginald's construction business was going bankrupt.

And now Reginald was dead, poisoned at just the same time that his construction company was going bankrupt. He had died from same poison that had been found in Madison's locker, the waitress with whom he had an affair. And now Corbin's construction company was about to make a lot of money.

Belle's heart raced. Perhaps Madison was speaking the truth. Perhaps she had nothing to do with Reginald's death, after all. Perhaps Reginald's death had more to do with his business affairs than his love life.

Could this project be so important that someone was willing to kill him over it?

It would be easy to frame an employee of a winery for serving poisoned wine.

Belle frowned, recalling how Sheriff Barnes had told her not to leave town. Whoever had killed Reginald had not only tried to frame

Madison, but they had also cast suspicions on her, Belle Beaumont! After all, Belle was the one serving Reginald the champagne that had ultimately delivered the poison into the poor man.

She quickly set out the last of the coffee cups, her hands trembling slightly. Finally, all of the coffees were set out and Belle could no longer pretend that she had something to do. She reluctantly left the conference room and hurried back to the kitchen, her head in a whirl.

Could Corbin have planned all of this?

Corbin seemed quite calm and collected for someone who had lost a brother less than a month ago. Cold and business-like, even.

Belle reached the kitchen and sat down in a spare chair with a thump. "They must plan on building a bigger hotel on the winery grounds," Belle muttered to herself, remembering the map that she had seen on the presentation. "Corbin must be planning on some major investment if he's involved with it."

Tyler was already in the kitchen, drinking a cup of coffee himself. He looked at her shocked face and assumed that her thoughts were running along the same lines as his. "You look like you've seen a ghost," he said. "What do you think all that was about?"

Belle told him what she had seen in the conference room.

Tyler's mouth turned downwards and he shrugged. "Sounds to me like they may make changes around here." He looked worried. "I hope that it doesn't mean I'll be out of a job."

"I'm sure that's not what it means," said Belle, frowning. "It probably just has something to do with the winery. Maybe they're planning on expanding."

She wondered how much Reginald knew about this new project before he died.

Chapter 17

"And then, after we listened to the presentation on how to make jam, Wilma turned around to the rest of us, and you'll never guess what she said!" Grace Beaumont chattered on, as she dished up two plates of pasta. It was made with her secret tomato sauce recipe and smelled like heaven.

It was Friday, and Belle's grandmother had cooked lasagna, the ultimate comfort food. Belle was looking forward to it after a busy week of work at the winery.

Six days had passed since Madison had been taken in for questioning. The police hadn't formally charged her, but they had told her not to leave town. Madison had been in quite a state all week, and Belle was relieved to be away from her.

"What did she say?" Belle asked, as she helped Grace carry the plates over to the kitchen table.

"She said 'One date with Belle and she turned my nephew gay,'" Grace replied, as she took her seat at the head of the table.

"Are you serious?" Belle let out a chortle of laughter. "That's hilarious."

Clearly Edward, true to his word, had told his Aunt Wilma that she was dating a fellow called Tom. And, as expected, she appeared to be in flat denial.

"I know, right?" Grace chuckled. "So, I turned around to Wilma and told her that Edward had been gay since he was born. Everyone in town knew it."

Belle smiled. "And what did she say?"

"Well, it's true." Grace shrugged. "It's why I was quite alright with you going out on a date with him. I knew you two would end up friends."

"You could have told me he was gay, you know," said Belle through a mouthful of lasagna. "I don't remember much about him. And it would have saved both of us a lot of confusion and embarrassment."

"Oh, I know. But where's the fun in that?" Grace smiled mischievously at Belle. "I got a lovely bit of gossip out of it, though," she continued.

"What?" Belle asked, curious to know what it could be.

Grace's eyes twinkled. "Well, after the Guild meeting, I popped into Smith's Grocery Store, and I happened to bump into Edward there. So, I had to congratulate him on how well he's doing working in the city and then, of course, for telling his aunt to let him set up his own dates. He said that he only felt brave enough to do so because you had encouraged him."

Belle's eyes widened in surprise. "Really?" She was touched that Edward had actually listened to her. "What did he say after that?"

"Oh, just how wonderful his boyfriend is. Some investment banker, apparently," Grace said. "He's going to introduce him to Wilma this weekend."

"Wow," Belle replied, impressed that Edward had followed through with her advice and done something about it. "I hope they will be really happy together."

Grace smiled. "Me too, dear. Me too. It's so nice to see people being happy. Not like that billionaire fellow flirting with everyone. I heard that he was even flirting with a waitress up at the winery, for heaven's sake. And that's on top of flirting with you on New Year's Eve."

Belle cringed, thinking about how her night with Reginald had turned out. "You didn't tell Edward, did you?"

"I did. He said that if he ever saw his boyfriend, Tom, flirting with someone else, that person would be dead, too," Grace replied casually as she took another mouthful of lasagna. "You're lucky that you didn't get poisoned. *If* she poisoned Reginald, of course."

"Thanks, Gram, that's very helpful," said Belle, rolling her eyes. "Is it possible to ever keep a secret in this town?"

"I don't know what you're complaining about," Grace replied. "I'm pretty sure everyone knows about you dancing with Reginald, the not-so-rich-billionaire, by now. And kissing him at midnight."

Belle sighed. "Oh, don't remind me. Is it too late to hide under a rock?"

"Afraid so," Grace said. "I think Madison is probably hiding under one at the moment."

Belle helped herself to more lasagna. "Madison isn't very nice to be around, but I don't think that she's capable of poisoning someone."

"I don't know, dear. I haven't even met the girl. But it sounds like she's the only person who would have the motive to do something like that."

Belle thought for a minute. Something about the story her Gram relayed had stuck in her brain. "Wait a minute, could you repeat what Edward told you?" she asked.

"Oh, of course," Grace replied, putting her knife and fork on the table. "He said Tom was an investment banker and that he was going to introduce him to Wilma next weekend."

"No, the bit about if he saw his boyfriend flirting with someone."

Grace thought for a moment. "Oh, that's right. He said if he caught his boyfriend flirting with someone else on New Year's Eve, that person would be dead."

Belle's heart rate picked up. Grace had just given Belle an idea, and she wasn't sure why it hadn't occurred to her before.

She took a deep breath and said, "Exactly! Madison was crazy jealous of me dancing with Reginald. And then when she found out he wasn't as rich as he was pretending to be, she was even more furious. But that's because she genuinely loved him, don't you think?"

Grace's eyes widened. "Well, I thought she just wanted his money—"

"That's not true," Belle replied. "She told me she would have given up the money if he had been honest with her from the beginning."

"Oh my," Grace said, putting a hand to her chest. "How romantic."

"And like Edward said, if you're in love with a person, and you see them flirting with someone else, you're more likely to be angry at the interloper, don't you think?"

"I suppose so," Grace replied.

Belle smiled triumphantly and kissed her grandmother on the cheek. "Thank you so much, Gram. I think that you've helped me solve a piece of this puzzle."

"Well, that's good to hear, darling," she replied, pushing a piece of hair out of her eyes. "I love you too. Now, will you clear away these plates and put the kettle on? I need my tea. Thank you, my dear."

As Belle put the kettle on, she revised what she knew about the murder of Reginald Hartford. A flirty billionaire who wasn't as rich as he had seemed and who had met his end at a party for the rich and famous. Had a jealous server poisoned the man for flirting with another person, and then hid the incriminating evidence in her locker? It all seemed a little too convenient to Belle, and something wasn't adding up.

"Right, Gram," Belle said as she put two mugs down on the table and took a seat next to her grandmother. She had not forgotten that Sheriff Barnes had told her not to leave town, either. The fact that she was the last person to serve Reginald wine didn't look good for her. "I think that we need to figure out who killed Reginald."

"Oh, really?" Grace replied, lifting her eyebrows. "And how are we going to do that?"

"Well, Madison is no murderer."

"What makes you so sure?"

Belle let out a deep sigh. "Well, the whole thing about Reginald's death just doesn't feel right. He was poisoned, but everything points to Madison as his killer."

"I know," Grace said. "But we don't have an alternative explanation for who killed him."

"Nope," Belle replied, "but while Madison had the motive and the opportunity, poisoning Reginald doesn't seem like the actions of a jealous woman who was very much in love."

"Well, I'm not sure what it means," Grace said. "It's possible Madison was framed, or maybe she's hiding a secret."

Belle nodded and took a sip of tea. "There's something about the fact that Reginald was pretending to be wealthy that still bothers me. If he had told Madison that he wasn't as wealthy as she thought, I think things could have gone differently. But he didn't. Why was he hiding it?"

"Probably because he was embarrassed and enjoyed being featured in magazines as the one of the most eligible bachelors in the world." Grace was very matter-of-fact.

Belle frowned. "Yes, but I think there may be more to this."

"More? like what?"

Belle paused for a moment before speaking. "Well, it's something that I remember from the night of the party. Mr. Buchen told me to serve all the *paying* customers. And he looked like he really didn't like Reginald. Maybe he meant Reginald wasn't a proper paying customer."

Grace thought for a moment. "Honey, I think that's probably because Mr. Buchen is always like that." She paused, scratching her chin. "Hang on! You don't think that your boss *knew* that Reginald was only pretending to be rich?"

Belle nodded slowly. "I think that it's possible."

"But how would Mr. Buchen know that?"

Belle's face took on a determined expression. "I have no idea. But I intend to find out. Before Sheriff Barnes starts questioning me again."

Chapter 18

Belle arrived at the winery on Monday morning with a sense of purpose. She just wished that she had a plan of action. There was only a week left of work at the winery, and she really needed to figure out what to do to clear her name before her time at the winery ended.

She headed into the kitchen, waving a friendly hello to the chef, Mrs. Blatherwick. In her brief month there, Belle had made friends with all the kitchen staff.

"Hello, my dear! How are you?" Mrs. Blatherwick asked. "I have some fresh blueberry scones baked this morning if you'd like one." She offered her a tray that was piled high.

"I'll take one. Thank you so much!" Belle said gratefully, reaching for a scone and getting stuck in right away. "Mmm... that's delicious! Mrs. Blatherwick, you certainly are the master of baking. Do you have any special recipes that I can ask for?"

The chef shook her head. "Nonsense, dear, that's just one of my old recipes. And it's a trade secret." She winked and smiled warmly at Belle and then began stirring a big pot on the stove. "We're going to miss your friendly smile around the place."

"Oh, no! I'm still working here for another week at least," Belle said, her mouth half full of scone.

"I know, dear, but the work will be so quiet without you!" She nodded at Belle and then went back to stirring her pot. "Just remember that I'm always here if you need anything, okay?" she said.

"Thank you so much!" Belle said and took another bite of the scone.

Belle left the kitchen in search of Madison, who was out in the wine cellar. "Hi, Madison," she said, spotting a flash of auburn hair at the bottom of stairs that led into the wine cellar. "I meant to ask if you found out anything new from the police when they questioned you last week."

"Yes, I talked to one of the police officers," Madison said coldly, coming up the stairs. She was holding an empty crate. "I told him again what I already said at the station. I know nothing else, sorry." She shrugged and reached for another wine bottle on a shelf after brushing the dust off it.

Belle spotted a bottle of wine she had never seen before. "What's this?" she asked, examining the label.

"It's an 'eiswein.' It's very sweet and good paired with fruit or cheese. The grapes used to make it are frozen while they're still on the vine," Madison explained, putting the bottle into the crate. "It's very expensive too. I think the owner saved it for a special occasion. He told me to bring it in for a couple of important customers today. It was Reggie's favorite."

She looked very sad all of a sudden.

"I'm sure it was," Belle said, averting her eyes from looking at Madison. She knew how sensitive she was about Reginald's death. "So... the police don't have any other leads? They told me not to leave town either, you know. Although, why they think a couple of waitresses would have killed a billionaire, I have no idea. I don't think Sheriff Barnes has much to go on at the moment."

"Yeah. I don't think they know anything, but the sheriff was quite nice to me, actually. Just like you have been," Madison said, glancing at Belle and giving her a small smile. "He seems to be good at his job. I'm sure they'll solve this case soon. They're looking into Reggie's business deals too. We both know now that he was involved in some shady stuff and lost a lot of money."

"That's what I think too. Maybe that's why he was killed," Belle agreed carefully, taking the last bite of her scone and licking the crumbs off her fingers as she spoke. Her experience of Madison had taught her to tread carefully around her.

Madison looked at Belle with sad eyes. "I've been a bit of a wasp to everyone, haven't I?"

"Well, yes, actually," Belle said, keeping a careful distance. "But I'm still sorry all this has happened to you and Reginald."

"Thank you, Belle," Madison said with a sigh and a shaky smile. "I'm sorry that I was rude to you. I've liked you from the beginning, you know, but I was so upset about Reggie. First, with him flirting with you. Then he died, and then I found out he had been lying to me. I shouldn't have treated you the way I did."

Belle nodded in acknowledgment of the other woman's apology and stood up. She brushed off her skirt as she spoke. "No, you shouldn't have. But let's move on. We need to figure out who did this to Reginald, so we can clear both of our names once and for all. Let's check people's lockers."

Belle headed to the staff room, Madison in tow. It was where the police had found the little bag of white powder, after all. It seemed like the logical place to start.

"Belle, I don't know if this is a good idea," Madison said as they approached the door. "It wasn't either of us. Why would we want to snoop around in there in other people's lockers?"

"We need to do something!" Belle insisted.

Just then, they overheard someone passing in the corridor. Belle pulled Madison into the staff room, while they waited for whoever it was to pass by. Belle peeked around the doorway to see who it was and noticed the back of Mr. Buchen receding down the corridor. He was speaking on the phone. The words "... but I invested the most. Hartford owed me..." floated back.

She couldn't make out his next words, but he sounded upset.

Belle quickly shut the door and turned back to Madison, a look of shock on her face. "Reginald owed *Mr. Buchen* money?" she asked in disbelief.

Madison looked just as shocked. "Reginald was always going on about how his business deals were going to make him a fortune. Last year, he was often in this area on business. That's how I got to see him so much."

It suddenly all seemed a little too coincidental. Belle's mind was racing. "Maybe the business in the area was with Mr. Buchen."

Madison nodded, a thoughtful look on her face. "Yes, I thought the fact that Reggie was here so often was strange too. Reggie made it sound as though he was meeting with clients here about their wines. Not that I complained. I was too busy enjoying his company." She flushed and looked down at the floor.

There was a clattering from down the hall, as the kitchen door opened and one of the kitchen staff came out carrying a basket full of clean dishes. They both drew into the staff room again, out of sight.

Madison frowned, as if trying to dredge up a memory. "I remember Reggie telling me that Mr. Buchen said he should merge one of his companies with the winery, so they could have an even bigger operation. Something about a new resort," Madison said. "But I thought Reggie was joking." The auburn-haired woman looked like she had just realized something.

"What if it wasn't a joke?" Belle asked her, remembering the detailed presentation that she had seen in the conference room. "What if he was really going to do it? Mr. Buchen could have paid him a lot of money to develop a resort on the winery and Reginald could have lost it. I think Mr. Buchen is a businessman, first and foremost. He might not have thought twice about getting revenge on your boyfriend."

Madison looked at her in astonishment. "Belle, you sound like you're accusing Mr. Buchen of killing Reginald!"

"I'm not accusing him of anything yet," Belle said, "But it's definitely worth looking into. It makes sense."

"I think you're getting carried away," Madison said. "What are we going to do? Ask him?"

Belle bit her lip. She hadn't thought about how they would go about investigating Mr. Buchen. "We could look in his office?" she suggested cautiously.

"But in a week or so, you aren't even supposed to be working here anymore!" Madison reminded her. "And if Mr. Buchen catches us, he might not take it well."

Belle had to admit Madison was probably right, but she didn't want to give up. "I really think we should try to figure this out while we can."

"Well, you can go ahead if you like," she said decisively. "I can't imagine why Mr. Buchen would want to kill Reginald. If he lent him money, it wouldn't exactly help to get it back, now, would it? I'm not getting more involved. It was nice knowing you, Belle."

Chapter 19

Deciding to sneak into her boss's office was one thing, but actually doing it was another. Belle paused in a little alcove at the top of the stairs leading to her boss's office, looking around for anyone who might see her. She thought she heard footsteps behind her, but perhaps that was just her overactive imagination.

Calming herself down, Belle breathed in and out a few times, then listened again. No footsteps.

The door to Mr. Buchen's office was closed.

Was he inside?

There was no way of knowing from where she was standing. The door had a sizeable gap at the bottom, and she was pretty sure that the light was off.

The last thing that she wanted to do was to sneak into her boss's office, while he was sitting at his desk. How would she explain that?

Oh, sorry, I didn't know you were in there. Just getting evidence of your potential involvement in a murder case.

It would not be the best way to make that sure she got her last paycheck.

After pausing for a moment to think, she did the most obvious thing and knocked on the door. If he was in there, she'd apologize and come back later. If he wasn't, then she could pop in quickly and look for evidence.

There was no answer. She knocked again, louder this time.

Still, there was nothing.

She glanced at her watch. It was eight minutes to ten o'clock. Mr. Buchen must have left on his daily rounds of the winery. He normally checked on the operations at this time of day.

She looked over her shoulder again, then ground her teeth in frustration.

Just do it. No point turning back now!

Belle turned the doorknob. It turned with little resistance, and she opened the door enough to slip through.

The office was dark, even in the light of day that came through the window behind Mr. Buchen's antique wooden desk. Belle turned on her phone flashlight and looked around. A large oil painting depicting the vineyard at sunrise hung on the wall to her left, and two smaller landscapes hung side-by-side on the right. The remaining the walls were covered with certificates and wine awards.

At the far end of the office stood a filing cabinet and a door that Belle assumed led to a washroom. The cabinet was dark wood with brass handles, the same as Mr. Buchen's desk and chair. On the desk was one of those old-fashioned in-and-out trays, a blotter, an expensive-looking desk lamp, a telephone, and a closed laptop. The chair was large and covered with red leather.

How do you hide incriminating papers in such a bare office?

Belle searched the desk drawers. She pulled open each of the center drawers of his desk. The first drawer had nothing but pens, pencils, and paperclips inside. The second one had empty files and business cards in it, so she closed it again.

The bottom drawer was locked tight. She tried to pry it open, but the metal lock held fast. After a few minutes of struggling with it, she gave up, turning her attention to the filing cabinet. It was locked, but the keys were conveniently placed on top of the cabinet. Belle pulled open one of the side drawers and lifted out files, looking for anything that would show financial transactions with Reginald Hartford or his company. The filing cabinet had four drawers full of files, all neatly labeled. The documents in each drawer appeared to date back years. She scanned the labels on each file, but didn't recognize any names.

As she pushed a large drawer of the filing cabinet back in, she heard the unmistakable tinkling sound of keys sliding about in the bottom. Moving the hanging folders to the side, she opened the drawer again and pulled out a small bunch of keys.

Two small keys on a ring.

Her eyes immediately traveled back to the desk, to the locked bottom drawer.

Hurrying back over to the desk, she tried the first key in the lock. It turned, and she pulled open the drawer. Inside was a folder full of documents and, at the very bottom, a closed manila envelope. She removed both and laid them on top of the desk.

She read the heading on the first document in the folder, mouthing the words as she read them,

Partnership Agreement.

It was between Mr. Buchen and Reginald Hartford. According to the document, Reginald Hartford was a silent partner in Buchen Wines. The winery had been struggling for years and could barely make ends meet, but with Mr. Hartford's help, they planned to establish a new vineyard and winery on land that Reginald had recently purchased. There were photos of the land and blueprints for a new building attached. It looked like some kind of luxury resort, with swimming pools and tennis courts and a health spa. Belle looked through them quickly, then placed them back inside the folder.

She turned her attention to the envelope. It was sealed and there was no writing on it. She broke the seal and pulled out a stack of papers. After leafing through them quickly, she realized it was a life insurance policy on Reginald Hartford.

His beneficiary was listed as... Mr. Buchen. Belle's heart skipped a beat when she saw how much money the policy was made out for.

Ten million dollars!

She read quickly, her eyes scanning the page. If anything happened to Reginald while the property deal was underway, or in five years after that, Mr. Buchen would inherit the money from his insurance policy. The policy had been taken out a few months ago. Belle wondered why Mr. Buchen would have needed to take out an insurance policy on his partner's life if he was investing heavily in the business. Was the investment that risky?

A newspaper clipping was included in the papers, and some words in it were circled in red ink, as if Mr. Buchen had been highlighting them. Belle read it:

A new resort is due to be built on a large patch of land near the coast, owned by a local billionaire, Reginald Hartford. However, construction work has been delayed somewhat because of the resort construction company, Hartford International Holdings, filing for bankruptcy because of its crushing debts to its investors.

At the bottom of the article was a photo of Reginald Hartford standing in front of an excavator, hands on his hips. He wore a debonaire smile, a white shirt, and a large, dark-brown Stetson hat. He looked like the carefree fellow who had danced with her at the New Year's Eve party. Belle marveled that someone could have been so relaxed when they were in such financial difficulty. She shook her head. And there she had been worrying about paying for her grandmother's medical bills! They were tiny compared to whatever Reginald Hartford had been going through.

So, Reginald had owed so much money to investors that his companies were going under. And Mr. Buchen had taken out an insurance policy on Reginald in case Reginald died during the construction of his new resort?

As she opened the folder again, a small plastic packet fell onto the desk. She picked it up, staring at the thick white powder inside. It looked exactly like the packet found in Madison's locker, and Belle was willing to bet that it contained the same substance. Arsenic.

"Oh dear," Belle said to herself. "What have you done, Mr. Buchen?"

Belle held her breath as she pulled out her phone and snapped photos of the packet and the documents, then she shoved it back into the envelope and the folder where she found it. She shoved all the papers back into the drawer, turning the key in the antique lock.

But it refused to lock!

She must have turned the key the wrong way. She tried turning it the other way, and it still didn't work.

Then she heard a creak on the landing outside the office door and froze. She looked at her watch. It was too early for Mr. Buchen to be back from his rounds. She heard another creak, then silence. Someone must have been standing outside the door listening!

The creaking stopped. Belle's heart raced as she fumbled with the key again.

Heavy footsteps sounded outside. The office door opened before she could hide.

Mr. Buchen stood in the doorway, and he didn't look happy.

Chapter 20

"What are you doing in here?" asked Mr. Buchen in a dangerously low voice, closing the door behind him. He pushed the internal latch shut, locked the door, and withdrew the key, pocketing it.

Belle's hand went to her mouth.

"I... I... I'm sorry, Mr. Buchen. I was just..." she stammered. But she had no story prepared. She cursed her stupidity for not thinking up an excuse in advance.

"Just what? Hmm?" he said, advancing on her with an ominous look in his eyes. "You know very well that this room is strictly out of bounds!" The smile he usually reserved for guests to the winery was gone, and Belle realized with a sinking feeling that he could harm her in this office, and no one would be the wiser.

His eyes swept the room, noticing where she was standing behind the desk and the keys in her hand.

"Please don't tell me you let yourself into my locked desk," he said, his voice cold and flat. He advanced into the room.

"I'm so sorry, but I was curious to learn more about... wines. I came down here to ask you about something, and the door was open." She stepped backward around the desk, keeping it between them as he approached her.

Belle looked at the desk for something, anything, that she could use to defend herself if need be. Then she felt the lump in her pocket that was her phone and extracted it. She slid it out into her hand.

"You've no right to be in here without permission, Miss Belle," he said. "Spying on your employer is not only unprofessional, but also highly inappropriate. And I won't tolerate an invasion of my privacy." He was approaching the desk now. She could smell his aftershave from across the room. "Whatever it is that you think you know," he said, leaning forward menacingly. "You're wrong."

Belle moved around the side of the desk, keeping the piece of furniture between them. She lifted her chin defiantly. Holding up her phone, she pressed the screen and began to record a video of Mr. Buchen.

"I'm not wrong," she said. "You killed Reginald Hartford. To make sure that you got your money back. The money that you lost on a real estate development."

He laughed out loud at her accusation, displaying small uneven teeth for a moment. "And how did I do that? How?"

Belle glanced at her phone to make sure it was recording. "By putting poison in a wineglass that you knew I would serve to Reginald. That night at the party. New Year's Eve. You must have been watching us, waiting for the right moment. And when he poured himself a glass of wine into the glass that *you* had pushed to the front of the counter... you knew what would happen. I'm just lucky that I didn't drink from that glass."

"Preposterous," he said, laughter in his voice. "You have no proof, Belle. This is all conjecture. Do you imagine that you're Miss Marple or Hercule Poirot trying to film me there on your little phone?"

Belle kept the large desk between them. "You poisoned Reginald, and then tried to blame it on Madison, didn't you?" She pressed back against the wall and felt behind her with her free hand to find the window. She felt it suddenly, a cold pane against her shaking fingers.

"Belle, you're delusional. You have no proof." He sighed. "I don't know what you think you saw at the party. Nothing happened that night except a few too many drinks for a rich playboy who was having an affair with a bad-tempered, red-haired waitress. Who will believe you? Accusing me of putting the bag of poison in her locker and then getting the police to come and find it?" He pulled a self-satisfied face, as if remembering how he had worked out his devilish plan. "That silly red-haired girl actually believed Reginald when he told her he would whisk her away from her life of serving tables like Cinderella. The little working people are so stupid."

Belle's knees buckled slightly at this revelation. He had been planning all of this for months? She kept feeling along the windowpane.

It is the only way out of this room. If I could just get it open...

"It's so sad, really," Mr. Buchen continued, his face suddenly taking on a dark expression. "How Reginald mismanaged his fortune. We could have made a lot of money together, but then he—, " He stopped as if suddenly remembering he was speaking out loud. "Whatever. There's no way that I'm going to lose everything I've built at the winery."

"So, that's why you killed him?" she asked, casting a desperate glance at the door behind Mr. Buchen.

He snorted. "Do you think that I'm going to admit that to you, one of my employees, while you're recording me on your phone? How stupid do you think I am?"

Belle glanced back at the screen of her phone. She had Mr. Buchen right in the center of the screen and had recorded everything he said. "You won't get away with this, you know," she said, her voice trembling. "I have recorded everything you said."

He narrowed his eyes. "Like I said, nothing that you can use. But you're right about one thing. You're a problem that I hadn't expected to deal with. But I don't think that you'll be a problem for long. You're fired. Why don't you give me that phone now?"

Belle felt for the window latch and flicked it. It was too high to climb out of the window and down to the ground floor, but at least if she opened it, she could try to climb out onto a ledge on the side of the building or something. She remembered what the building looked like from the outside. It had quite a lot of facia work that might give her some grip. She could work her way around the side of the building and then down to ground level. It was a long drop, but maybe if she got really close to the ground, it wouldn't hurt too much to jump.

"Give me that phone, Belle." Mr. Buchen gave her a menacing look.

Just then, the phone rang. A photo of Grace Beaumont in her hair curlers instantly replaced the active video of Mr. Buchen in front of her. It was her grandmother, and she was trying to FaceTime.

Her boss took the opportunity of Belle's distraction to lunge for her, grabbing at her arm. Belle screamed and spun away from him, shoving the window open and leaning out. The vibrating phone slipped out of her hand and landed on the carpet, sliding under the desk, its face still illuminated with the photo of Grace in hair curlers.

Mr. Buchen dived for the phone, reaching out for it with his right hand, the other one still gripping Belle's arm.

She pulled her arm back quickly, wrenching herself free even as she leaned precariously out of the window. Climbing onto the windowsill, she grabbed the top of the window frame and swung out, her feet flailing for a foothold.

Through the phone, Grace could be heard speaking loudly, "Belle? Are you in an elevator? All I can see is wood paneling."

Belle's feet found a foothold and she frantically shuffled along a narrow ledge, while clinging to the building. Her boss leaned out of the window after her, reaching for her feet. She kicked down at him with all her might, dislodging a pile of snow from the window ledge that fell to the ground far below.

Suddenly, she slipped and found her feet scrabbling for another foothold on the facade of the building. She found one and leaned into it, pressing her chest against the freezing wall of the winery building. Her heart raced, adrenaline coursing through every vein in her body, as she stared down at the snow-covered ground far below.

"Belle, I can't tell what that screaming is. I think I may have the wrong number..." Grace was calling from the phone on the floor inside the office.

"You foolish girl," said her boss, leaning out of the window and failing to reach her. "You know that you can't stay there all night? You're going to fall, eventually."

Belle's fingers were already becoming numb in the cold, and she knew that he was right.

His head withdrew from the window momentarily and she heard the crunching sound of glass at the same time as the voice of her grandmother stopped speaking. She heard him exhale, and then he sighed.

His head reappeared. "I would normally say you would need to get a new phone, but I don't think you'll need it."

She took a deep breath as she felt herself slipping. He had destroyed her phone and with it, all the evidence that she had gathered. Her stomach clenched. What was she going to do now?

Just then, a siren sounded up the drive and Belle could see the flash of lights. She craned her neck.

It was a police squad car racing up the driveway of the winery.

Chapter 21

Belle clung to the creaking window frame with her increasingly numb fingers, as the police squad car disappeared out of sight around the side of the building. "Oh, thank goodness," she whispered.

Mr. Buchen had clearly heard the siren too because his head disappeared back inside the office, muttering curses. Before long, there was the sound of pounding on the office door.

"Open up, Mr. Buchen. This is the police," came the muffled shouts of Sheriff Barnes.

A few more pounding thumps of the door, and then there was the sound of crashing as the office door lock gave way.

"Don't move! You're under arrest," said someone who sounded like Officer Derek.

Belle inched back along the ledge to the windowsill just in time to see Sheriff Barnes grabbing Mr. Buchen's upper arms while Officer Derek handcuffed him.

Madison appeared. She rushed over to the window and helped pull Belle back inside the room. Belle's muscles ached from the tension of holding herself up and from the cold. She shivered in relief as she climbed back off the windowsill.

Madison quickly closed the window and latched it. "Are you okay?"

Belle nodded, as she rubbed her fingers to get the feeling back into them. "Thank goodness Sheriff Barnes got here in time. I think if he had been a minute longer, I would have fallen into the flowerbeds!"

Madison nodded and looked worried. "I'm so sorry that I didn't come in here with you. As soon as I saw Mr. Buchen come back from his rounds, I tried to slow him down in the hallway by talking to him about the inventory," she said, "But he was in such a hurry. When I saw him go into his office before you had come out, I called the police. They were already in the area inspecting something, so they weren't far away."

Belle walked over to the desk and collapsed into a chair. "Thank goodness you did! He killed Reginald, you know. I almost got him to admit it and I even recorded it all on my phone, but then he broke it." She realized she was standing on a broken bit of her phone and picked it up sadly.

Officer Derek led a defeated-looking Mr. Buchen away, out of the office, and down the stairs.

"Yes, I heard all of that," said Madison, raising her eyebrows. "And I recorded it too."

"What?" Belle jumped up. "But how?"

Madison reached into her pocket and pulled out her own phone. "I called the police then I ran up the stairs and slid my phone under the door as soon as Mr. Buchen closed it," she said, triumphant. "I recorded everything that happened in this room. Then, while it was recording, I went over there," she pointed to the other wing of the building. "I watched everything from the conference room balcony. Saw you climbing out of the window. You're nuts." She shook her head, a wry smile on her lips.

Belle laughed. "I know, but I had to find out the truth."

"And you did." Madison nodded.

Sheriff Barnes stepped toward them. "Are you okay, Belle?" he asked "You're lucky that you didn't fall. What you did was dangerous. We saw you hanging out of the window, as we drove up the driveway."

Belle nodded. "I'm fine," she said, looking at him gratefully.

He coughed. "Did I hear you say that you recorded everything, Madison?" he asked, looking over at her. "I'll have to take a copy as evidence."

Madison nodded, handing her phone over. "Of course, here you go," she said, raising her chin. "This is for Reginald."

Sheriff Barnes gave Belle an amused look. "This seems like déjà vu, recording everything on a phone."

"And I think you'll find incriminating documents in that drawer there," said Belle, pointing at the bottom drawer in the desk. "It turns out Mr. Buchen had invested in Reginald's new resort development and took out an insurance policy on his life to protect his investment," she said. "And he was trying to frame Madison for Reginald's murder."

Sheriff Barnes was already pulling on some gloves and opening the bottom drawer of the desk. He looked inside and nodded, then turned to Belle. "I guess you were right when you said Reginald's wealth needed to be looked into," he said, pulling out a pile of documents and the folder Belle had looked at earlier. "You two ladies did some great work in bringing a killer to justice."

"And I think that you'll find there is a packet of poison in that folder too." Belle pointed at the folder.

Sheriff Barnes raised his eyebrows, as he opened the folder and a little plastic Ziploc bag fell out onto the desk. "I'll make sure that this is tested," he said, picking it up in his gloved hand and shaking his head slightly. "It looks like you've solved another murder, Belle. Perhaps you should consider a change of career." He gave her a quizzical look.

"I think right now, I'm just glad it's all over." Belle sighed, shooting Madison a relieved look. "Perhaps we should crack open a bottle of champagne!"

Chapter 22

Grace put the apple pie on the kitchen table and the scent of baked sweet pastry, spiced apple, and cinnamon filled the kitchen. She had also baked some gingerbread cookies, which were on a plate decorated with royal icing. The winter chill had come in early that day and the fire in the fireplace had already been lit.

Doris, Grace's friend from the Women's Guild, finished whipping the cream and brought it to the table too, in a large and fancy jug. Several plates and forks were already waiting on the checked tablecloth. Mittens had shown great interest in the jug of cream, and so Belle had distracted him with some healthy cat-chew treats.

"Oh, my goodness," Tom groaned with delight when he saw the pie. "Wow! You should set up a cafe with those home baking skills." He clutched his chest dramatically.

Tom-the-investment-banker turned out to be nothing like Belle had expected. When Edward had announced that he was taking her up on her offer of apple pie, and that he would bring Tom too, she had imagined someone in a dark blue suit. Nothing could be further from the truth. Tom wore Hawaiian shirts, tight jeans with a wide belt, and cowboy boots. His teeth were white and perfectly straight, and his dark eyes twinkled merrily.

"Gram refuses to sell her baked goods, unless it's for charity." Belle chuckled at Tom's faux-heart attack over the pie.

"Thank you for inviting us," said Edward to Belle, glancing at his Aunt Wilma who was organizing the plates and forks and chattering to Grace about the best way to slice pie.

"Of course! It's lovely to have company and to meet Tom," Belle replied. "What a way to start the year. My ex-boss, Mr. Buchen, has been formally arrested for the murder of Reginald Hartford. It's all over the local news."

Doris shook her head. "Thank goodness they caught the murderer of that handsome billionaire. Although it's a bit boring now that he isn't in the gossip mags anymore."

"I know," Belle said. "Poor guy. He never deserved what happened to him. Who would have thought Mr. Buchen would turn out to be a scheming murderer?"

Wilma tutted and handed Belle a plate of pie. "I did. Always thought that he was a dodgy person. A terrible person to have living here in Cherryville all this time." She flicked her short hair over her shoulder.

"No, you didn't," said Grace stoutly. "You said he was very important to the town and shouldn't have bad press." She put her hands on her hips and raised her eyebrows.

"And wasn't it you who was standing next to him in that expensive dress in all the photos from the exclusive New Year's Eve party at the winery?" chimed in Doris, assuming an innocent expression.

"Well, yes. But never mind that. What's more important is what do you all think of my new hairstyle? Tom told me that I needed to frame my face better and wear more pink." She flicked her highlighted hair again and struck a bit of a pose in a hot pink knitted top.

"He's right," said Grace. "It does suit you better. Didn't I tell you something similar last year when we got our colors done by that lady who did a presentation at the Women's Guild?" It had been for a local fundraiser, and they had hired an ex-beauty queen who had branched into the business of color analysis.

"Did you? I don't remember," declared Wilma, sitting down and waving a dismissive hand. "I'm going to get Tom to help me choose the new curtains for my lounge this weekend. That way, we can make sure that they go with the carpet."

Belle watched as Edward and Tom exchanged an amused glance. Tom had sat down opposite Belle and he leaned across the table, his eyes shining mischievously. "I'm going to help Aunt Wilma pick a new carpet for her lounge room too." He dropped his voice to a whisper and spoke behind his hand. "To replace that green monstrosity that she currently has installed in three rooms."

Belle laughed again. It seemed that Tom was a hit in the Figg household. She glanced at Edward, and he looked quite pleased as well. Belle wondered if Wilma knew what she was in for when it came to redecorating her house.

"And what is this?" asked Wilma, gazing at the bottle of dessert wine that Grace was busily opening with a corkscrew, the tip of her tongue poking out the side of her mouth in concentration. Finally, the cork popped out with a satisfying thwack. "Is that wine? This early in the day?"

"It is," said Gram proudly. "Tell them what it is, Belle."

"A gift from Madison," said Belle. "It's a very rare vintage of eiswein. It's got notes of pear and pineapple. A light dessert wine." She raised her eyebrows impressively and gave everyone a wide smile. "I'm almost a wine expert now. Almost."

"Speaking of wine experts, how is Madison these days?" asked Grace, as she poured six glasses of the deep gold liquid and passed them around.

Mittens, curious about what was happening at the table, had jumped onto Belle's lap and had started purring, his eyes fixed on the jug of cream. She stroked his head and scratched his chin. "I think that she's doing okay. More than okay, actually. She enrolled at a wine-making course across the country and is having the time of her life. I think she has plans to manage a winery one day."

"Good for her," said Doris approvingly. "Who needs a man, anyway?"

"That's really nice for her," agreed Grace, as she took a sip of the wine and gave an approving nod. "Hasn't this got a lovely flavor to it?"

"It has!" agreed Edward, eating another bite of apple pie. "It's delicious."

Doris finished her pie and pointed to her phone before placing it back in her pocket. "What are you going to do about a phone, Belle, since Mr. Buchen stomped on your last one? I guess you'll need a new phone."

Belle shrugged. "Yes, I guess I'll have to get a new one. The phone number stays the same, doesn't it?"

"Yes, but you need to make sure that you get Bluetooth enabled, a personalized lock screen, and cloud back-up." Doris nodded as she patted her pocket. "Goodness knows what could happen with your contacts list otherwise."

"How do you know about stuff like that?" asked Belle, wrinkling her nose. "I don't even know that stuff. And I'm at least thirty-five years younger than you."

"I watch a lot of educational videos online," said Doris, as she took another sip of her wine and helped herself to more pie. "I had no idea how many of them featured cats doing funny things, though."

Gram snorted. "Well, you can do what you like with your phone, but I've decided I'm never using FaceTime again. It freaks me out. I'm just going to phone people the old-fashioned way. It's a lot less stressful." She made a comical face. "And I got tired of speaking to a live video of Doris' ear."

Everyone laughed.

"So, what's going to happen about the new resort up the coast that Mr. Hartford was going to build?" asked Edward, when they quietened down again and he looked around the table. "Is someone else going to take it on? I heard that Corbin Hartford is not interested anymore. It seems sad for that project not to go ahead. It promised loads of new jobs for the residents of the county. And, before the previous construction company went bust, it looked like there had been a lot of investor interest."

Tom cleared his throat. "Well, actually, Edward, I'm pleased to announce that I've talked with investors in New York about taking it on. The winery is going to be sold to new owners for quite a low price. They aren't as big players as the initial investors, but they're interested. So, let's say things are looking positive." There were nods of agreement around the table and Tom continued. "We've already started talking to the town planners, county planners, and contractors. There are some details to be ironed out, but we have a good team working on it. I think that everything is going to work itself out."

"Thank goodness for that," declared Wilma, looking relieved. "I daresay that there will be many people who will be pleased to hear that. I say we start the new year again. We can't let that horrible Mr. Buchen spoil things for us. Now that he's going to jail, let's start the year again."

"Hear, hear," said Grace, raising her glass to Belle, and everyone followed suit. "To new beginnings!"

"And to new partners," said Doris loudly, refilling her glass already.

"And to new curtains," sang Wilma merrily.

"Ten... nine... eight..." started Edward, as Tom joined in the chant.

"Seven... six... five... four...three, two, one! HAPPY NEW YEAR!" they all yelled.

"And so it is," said Belle, as she looked around the table and smiled to herself. While no one was looking, she scooped a small dollop of cream onto a plate and passed it to a happy Mittens under the table. "So, it is indeed."

Chapter 23

Victims and Valentine's Day - Coming soon!

February in Cherryville, is a freezing and snowy month. For the shortest day of the month, it sure feels like the longest. Everyone stays indoors as much as possible and only the snowploughs are out every day. For many people, this could be the most boring and depressing time of year. The Christmas season is over and the year is no longer new.

But in Cherryville, there is one bright spot on the calendar: the Valentine's Day Ball.

An annual tradition for as long as the town had been founded, the Valentine's Day Ball had become something that everyone in town looked forward to. Held in the Town Hall on the fourteenth of February every year, it had become a fancy-dress extravaganza that was bigger and more spectacular with each passing year. This year was no different, and the whole town was abuzz with excitement in the weeks leading up to the big night.

"We are going to have a red carpet and everything," exclaimed Doris, clapping her hands, her grey curls bouncing. "The theme is going to be Hollywood Glamour. Just think of the possibilities!"

Doris had come for Sunday afternoon tea and cake, ostensibly to check on Grace Beaumont's health, but she already knew that her friend was doing well. What she had really come to do was to gossip about the upcoming Valentine's Day dance. Doris worked as the town seamstress for prom balls, weddings and other formal gatherings. The Valentine's Day Ball was one of her busiest times of year.

"That sounds like fun," said Grace, putting down her knitting and sitting back comfortably in her recliner. She turned to Belle. "Have you decided whether you are going to go to the Valentine's Day ball yet?"

"I'm not planning to go, no," said Belle. "I don't have anyone to go with. Remember? Or anything to wear. I would rather just stay home, anyway."

While the Ball was technically one of the highlights of Cherryville's social season, it was an event that Belle was more than happy to miss. She was particularly keen to miss the awards ceremony at the end. The awards always went to the same people every year: Gus and Barbara Fitzgibbon were usually named as Cherryville's Valentine's couple and Wilma Figg usually got the prize for the best-dressed. Belle rolled her eyes at the thought of it.

"Who cares about that?" said Grace, "You can go stag. You don't need a male to go to a party these days." She glanced at the cat. "No offence, Mittens."

Mittens jumped to the floor and started washing his paws, sublimely indifferent. Then he proceeded to clean his backside.

Belle laughed.

"Nonsense! You can't not go," said Doris, shocked. "Everyone is going to be there. Tell you what, I will get my sister-in-law's cousin to go with you. It will be such fun. And I am sure that we can rustle up a dress from someone."

Belle sincerely doubted that it would be fun to go with a complete stranger to a dance that she didn't want to attend. She had no idea who Doris' sister-in-law's cousin was and didn't care to find out. Plus, the thought of wearing someone else's dress or even spending money on a new dress for one night of wear was beyond her. She had more important things to spend her money on, like Grace's medical bills.

"Thanks, Doris, but I don't really like dances anyway," said Belle, smiling politely. "They make me uncomfortable." She had managed to avoid attending last year's Ball and planned to do the same this year.

Everyone judging everyone else's outfit and the progress of their love life? No thanks!

"You can go with me, if you want," suggested her grandmother, wriggling her eyebrows. "I could go as your date. But I warn you, I like to dance the funky chicken."

Belle burst out laughing. "I don't think anyone dances the funky chicken anymore, Gram," she said.

"Is that a no?" asked Grace, grinning. "Okay, but if you change your mind, let me know. I am looking forward to it."

"Me too," said Doris. "Everything is so cold and depressing and it's something for us all to look forward to. I just love the excitement of the Valentine's Day Ball every year and think you would too. Wilma is making all the arrangements together with the women from the Hollydale Women's Craft Club."

"Wilma is organizing it? With her arch enemies from Hollydale? Well, in that case, I can't wait," said Belle, opening her eyes wide. "She's going to make it super-duper fancy."

Wilma was the President of the Women's Guild in Cherryville and she made sure that she was involved in the organizing of most of the town's social events. However, her approach to organizing was always so over-the-top that something inevitably went wrong. The only person who enjoyed Wilma's over-the-top plans was Wilma. And possibly Doris.

"She certainly will make the ball special," said Doris. "I hope you don't mind, but I already asked for you to be on the decorations committee. You are so good at coming up with ideas."

"Yes, Belle. What a great idea. You always make such lovely Christmas decorations every year," said Grace, nodding her head. "How easy would it be to make decorations for the Valentine's Day Ball?"

Belle groaned inwardly. She wanted nothing to do with the Ball, but she didn't have the heart to disappoint Doris who was gazing at her with such a hopeful expression.

"Sure, I'd love to help," said Belle politely.

"Wonderful!" exclaimed Doris clapping her hands together in glee. "The Hollydale women are lovely to work with. They are the ones that came up with the idea for the Hollywood theme. We're meeting this Wednesday afternoon to discuss what needs to be done."

"Wednesday? I'll see if I can make it. I have a few things to worry about at the moment," mentioned Belle, changing the subject. "I expect I will be at work."

Now that January was over, Belle's work as a wine server at the Buchen Winery had come to an end. Fortunately, she had some money saved, sufficient to pay for the upcoming medical bill for Grace that was due in a couple of days. But she needed to earn more money to keep them going.

"What are you going to do?" asked Doris, sipping her snowberry tea.

"I was thinking that I could get a job answering phones," said Belle. "They want someone at the police station and Sheriff Barnes said he would hire me. He said that they need someone to take non-emergency calls."

"Oh, that will be nice," said Grace. "Much better than serving wine to all those rich people at the winery. And you've always been good on the telephone."

"Answering the phone? Really? Isn't that what Shirley does?" exclaimed Doris. "I'm surprised that Sheriff Barnes wants to get rid of her." Shirley had worked at the police station for decades. Her voice was usually the first one that the people in town heard when they phoned for help.

"They don't want to get rid of her, Doris," corrected Grace. "Shirley is planning to retire soon. And she has to visit her daughter in California to help with her first grandchild. Shirley is going to train Belle and then Belle will take over."

"Shirley is planning to retire? That's surprising," said Doris, helping herself to some more of the purple berry cake that Grace had made. "I thought that she was planning on working forever, as you did."

Belle smiled at her grandmother. Grace had taught school for thirty-seven years until she retired a couple of years ago. She'd always planned to do something else when she retired, but then got her cancer diagnosis and was taking it easy after the treatment.

"Well, Shirley said that she would have stayed and worked longer. Now she is retiring early, and it is all happening a lot faster than she expected." Grace smiled. "She is so excited."

Everyone knew that Shirley's daughter was about to have her first baby any day now. It was all Shirley could talk about, at the grocery store, at church and to anyone who phoned the police station. Ever since her daughter's wedding, Shirley had been counting the days until she would be a grandmother.

"She says that Belle will be a splendid replacement for her. Belle is so cheerful. Plus, she already knows Sheriff Barnes well, and she went to school with his deputy, Derek," said Grace. "You said yes right away, didn't you Belle?"

"Well, I was just pleased that they were offering me a job," said Belle, sipping her tea. "I could use a desk job for a change and it sounds much better than being on my feet all day. I just hope that I'll be able to handle all the calls. I start tomorrow, Monday morning."

"You will do a great job," said Doris. "Sheriff Barnes is a lovely man. He was so good to me after my husband passed away a few years back. Kept checking that I was doing alright."

"Yes. Plus, I'm sure that you'll be great at whatever job you choose," agreed Grace, patting Belle's hand. "You're a smart girl, Belle."

"Sheriff Barnes and his wife always attend the Ball. Does that mean you will be coming, after all?" said Doris.

"No, but I will help with the decorations. Hollywood Glamour did you say?" said Belle, trying to change the subject, again. "Did you say that she is organizing it with the Hollydale ladies?"

Hollydale was the neighboring town and had a friendly rivalry with Cherryville when it came to events. They were always trying to outdo Cherryville, something that brought out the competitive side in most of the town residents, who wanted to win. Cherryville had come in second place at the annual Winter Jump a couple of years back and they had recently lost the area's Snowman Competition when the Cherryville team was bested by a snowman built on top of a moving snowboard, courtesy of the kids from Hollydale Elementary. The competitive spirit had been alive and kicking ever since.

"Yes! We are going to turn the town hall into an old-fashioned Hollywood nightclub. It'll be fun," said Doris, clapping her hands together. "What could go wrong?"

"What indeed?" replied Belle, trying not to let her imagination run away with her.

About the Author

Ellie McDougan is a pen name for an author who grew up in Africa, then studied and traveled a lot before settling down. This has come in handy for her writing, as she likes to include some elements of different countries in her mysteries. She writes about women who work in many different jobs yet seem to find themselves solving crimes at them all. If you love cozy mysteries with a touch of humor, you'll love her books!

Ellie now lives in Australia with three cats, all of which she adores. When she's not writing or spending time with her felines, she enjoys reading stories about solving crimes (of course), studying some more, starting slightly skewed sewing projects but never finishing them, and watching DIY videos on Youtube that no one should try at home. Trust her, she's tried them.

Read more at https://elliemcdougan.com/.

www.ingramcontent.com/pod-product-compliance
Lightning Source LLC
Chambersburg PA
CBHW071304130626
46556CB00003B/1462